Books by Mari Sandoz
published by the University of Nebraska Press

The Battle of the Little Bighorn
The Beaver Men: Spearheads of Empire
The Buffalo Hunters: The Story of the Hide Men
Capital City
The Cattlemen: From the Rio Grande across the Far Marias
Cheyenne Autumn
Christmas of the Phonograph Records
Crazy Horse: The Strange Man of the Oglalas
The Horsecatcher
Hostiles and Friendlies: Selected Short Writings of Mari Sandoz
Letters of Mari Sandoz
Love Song to the Plains
Miss Morissa: Doctor of the Gold Trail
Old Jules
Old Jules Country
Sandhill Sundays and Other Recollections
Slogum House
Son of the Gamblin' Man: The Youth of an Artist
The Story Catcher
These Were the Sioux
The Tom-Walker
Winter Thunder

The Horsecatcher

by MARI SANDOZ

University of Nebraska Press
Lincoln

First Bison Book printing: 1986

Library of Congress Cataloging-in-Publication Data
Sandoz, Mari, 1896–1966.
  The horsecatcher.
  "Bison book"
  Summary: Unable to kill, a young Cheyenne is scorned
by his tribe when he chooses to become a horse catcher
rather than a warrior.
  1. Cheyenne Indians—Juvenile fiction.
[1. Cheyenne Indians—Fiction. 2. Indians of
North America—Fiction. 3. Horses—Fiction] I. Title.
PZ7.S22Ho 1986   [Fic]   86-4360
ISBN 0-8032-4166-6
ISBN 0-8032-9160-4 (pbk.)

Reprinted by arrangement with The Westminster Press,
Philadelphia, Pennsylvania

∞

DEDICATED to the two great Cheyennes named Elk River, both council chiefs and peace men, one Keeper of the Sacred Arrows of the Cheyenne Indians, the other the greatest horse-catcher of all the High Plains.

1

*Y*OUNG ELK slipped along just under the crest of the ridges. He moved as the wolf travels, where he would not be silhouetted against the sky and yet where he could search the wide slopes of prairie on both sides, and vanish quickly in either direction if need be.

The young Indian was dressed to fade into the drying summer prairie, in a gray-figured calico trader's shirt, his braids wrapped in the calico too, his leggings and breechclout of deerskin, with sturdy Cheyenne moccasins and an extra pair tied to his back. He carried only a light bow and quiver, for around his waist was a thick coil of rope.

Several times the Elk glanced toward the scattered buffalo herd off to his left, browsing, resting along a little creek. He kept downwind from them so they would not catch his scent and be disturbed, probably run. No use making them wild for the hunters and perhaps signaling his presence to roving enemies. Besides, their flight would alarm his quarry, if anywhere near.

Cautiously the Cheyenne youth crept to look over a ridge, and forgot both the buffaloes and possible enemies. Small herds of wild horses dotted all the wide plain below him and as far westward as he could see. The closer ones grazed or stomped flies, the colts down sleeping or running in play, the far-off only small dark specks on the hazy summer prairie. As Young Elk looked from one herd to another, searching, the horses suddenly swept together like dark leaves in a gust of wind and then spread, all the plain moving, running. They could not have seen him, he knew. It must have been a wolf, perhaps, or a dry-weather whirlwind, or a rolling tumbleweed that frightened one horse to running, and so all went.

It must have been something small, perhaps only a rattlesnake's angry whirring, for the horses didn't run far. But they kept moving now and the Elk followed, edging in closer, creeping to one knoll after another, from weed to bush to washout until he located the little herd he sought, mostly mares, gray and bay, with a black and a sorrel, and their colts. He was very careful now, and swung around down a draw and ran to head them so if he must follow a long time, he would not be in some far enemy country.

The young Indian kept well hidden, but in the excitement of this first chase afoot and alone he ran too hard, without the judgment of a trained runner or the horse stalker's patience. Instead, his moccasins sang on the grass as though he could hope to outdistance any mustang before the next ridge. He ran until he was winded and his side ached as from the hot thrust of a Kiowa lance. Torn with the pain, he recalled an old Cheyenne remedy. Stooping far over to his left side without bending a knee, he picked up a pebble, spit under it, and replaced the little white stone into its exact nest. He smiled to himself as the pain eased off and he recalled that his grandmother was saved by this once, long ago. She had been fleeing from an enemy attack on the village, running with her small son on her back until the pain of her haste seemed a mortal wound. For all the whooping of the warriors behind her, she had to stoop down to lift the easing pebble — and saw

8

a hole like a low cave under the hang-over of grass at a washout. She crawled in there until the pursuers, too high up on their charging horses to see the hole, were safely past and night crept down the draw.

Fortunately Young Elk was hunting horses and not fleeing from enemies, at least not yet. With his side relieved a little, he decided to take a look over the next ridge. He wasn't far enough ahead of the little herd, his circling entirely too short, but he was pleased actually to see the colt that he had noticed two days ago on the way home with a party from a ceremonial. The colt was a very late one, just born then, and staggering to his feet, the mare old and not worth a chase, Elk's father had said — not even the short chase required to capture such a poor one. But the wobbly black foal had fine long legs and on one side a white patch shaped like a bear reaching from the rump forward to the shoulder, a big white patch like a bear running, flat paws lifted in his hurry up the withers.

Now Elk had found the colt again, but already much stronger, playfully jumping and shying around the restless mares. He wished he had his brother, Two Wolves, along, and fast horses. They could easily catch the whole little bunch and be much safer than Elk alone, afoot. It was true that the horses were not worth the chase and the taming, particularly so far in dangerous country, yet Young Elk had been drawn to the new foal by something beyond the value for use or trade. As he watched Bear Colt yesterday he had wanted, not to catch him, but to run beside him over prairie and hilltop, in sun and in the rain. There seemed something like a calling on the summer wind from the colt, a calling that made a gaiety and a softness within the breast of the young Cheyenne.

Overimpatient now that the colt was there before him, Elk started to crawl toward the resting horses. He moved carefully up along a low place, the grass as unstirred by his passing as from a snake's cautious glide. But he had no plan even if he got close enough for an arrow. Either he had to tire the horses out or shoot the mare if he could. Then the little foal would be easy to wear down by cutting across on him as a wolf does a rabbit. But while Elk was trying to overcome his deep reluctance to any killing, a bird flew up from among the mares. It was the shining black bird that rides on horses and picks insects and nits out of the long, ensnaring manes. In return it was a good watcher, as good a scout as any guarding a Cheyenne village.

The bird burst into the air with a sharp cry of alarm, and the horses were off again, past the young Indian, the mares with their heads up, manes and tails flying in a windy cloud about them, their colts running at their flanks. Behind them the gray stallion hurried the lagging old mare, threatening to nip his long teeth into her rump as soon as the chase got hot. Her young colt tried hard to keep up, the clean white side like a galloping bear.

Young Elk was angered by his foolish impatience. But there was nothing to do now except follow out upon the open prairie where he could be detected by enemies from very far off, with nowhere to run. He wished he might have approached Old Horsecatcher for advice before he left the village. But the Catcher was known as a great man among all the Cheyennes and the neighboring tribes; he was very wise in the ways of the wild herds, and in the capture of stock from enemies. When anyone wanted to go out for horses, he was consulted. It was Horsecatcher who laid the plans and told how everything could be done, but his wisdom was for well-organized parties of grown, experienced men, not for a lone untried youth like Young Elk, who had never struck an enemy or even killed a buffalo.

True, Elk had helped gentle the colts of the family herd

10

and several belonging to the father of Red Sleeve, pretending it was friendship for her brother and not because he hoped to turn the soft glances of the girl in his direction. Some said Elk was good with young horses, that he had the gentling hand, but this gave him no place among the admirers of the handsome Red Sleeve and certainly no right to approach the fire of Old Horsecatcher. Besides, it was known that there were war parties of Kiowas and Comanches out down this way, and some Utes too, and many of their hunters, all eager to kill or capture a young Cheyenne. No one would have given Elk permission to go, and so he had sneaked away in the gray sleep of dawn.

For a while Young Elk made himself remember these enemies as he followed the little herd, slipping through draws and gullies whenever he could. But he must keep the horses moving, for therein lay his vague hope of catching Bear Colt. He must give them no rest and no time to eat or to water night or day. It would be hard, for man also liked sleep, and Elk himself could sleep as soundly as the badger in his winter burrow. Unfortunately too, an Indian needed to eat and drink as much as the horses did, and the little waterskin now bobbing at Elk's belt and the bladder of pemmican that he had pilfered from his mother's store would not last long.

Several times he tried to get the little herd headed back toward his home region, but the long runs around them always gave the horses a little rest, and when he reappeared the wily lead mare just swung out past him and Young Elk had to run even harder to keep the herd from edging eastward to lower ground, where the creeks were not yet dry and where no lone pursuer could hope to keep them from watering.

As the sun began to move down the sky, Young Elk neared a scattering of buffaloes moving out from a string of late ponds that the horses tried to reach. The buffaloes caught a whiff of the man smell on the wind, and, lifting their ropy tails, followed their noses toward it, to discover the danger. The young Indian stopped as he had seen hunters do, ready to run cross-wind if the thundering animals came too close, for it was well known that the weak-eyed buffalo saw very little under that mat of hair on his forehead, but followed his nose instead.

When the buffaloes caught his smell clearly, they turned and were gone in a gallop over a rise. The horses stampeded too, but heading for some choppy breaks where there were probably seepage springs. Elk ran hard on legs that seemed broken with weariness. He managed to scare the horses from the live bogs under a bluff by slipping his shirt off and waving it, panting too much for a dangerous whooping in this place of wild things. Two deer ran from the marsh and ravens rose in their squawking while another herd of mustangs bolted, running, kicking their heels, fresh and full of vigor, drawing the weary horses on once more.

By now Elk was more than two sleeps of regular travel from where he first found Bear Colt again, better than forty of the white man's miles. Surely the lead mare would be circling back northward soon, to her usual range. Instead she headed straight on, and all the young Indian could do was to try to stay close enough to keep them moving, keep them from feed or rest and particularly from water.

Around dusk the herd began to lag and an excitement rose in Elk as he got his rope out to catch the little colt. But as he hurried to cut the distance, the rise of the late moon seemed to strengthen the horses, or perhaps it was the howling of the coyotes and wolves that echoed from ridge to ridge. Slowly the herd drew farther away, until they were only darkish blurs in the dusky moon. If they struck water, they could drink their fill before Elk was there —

Then suddenly he smelled smoke, the smoke of burning buffalo chips.

He was leaning his ear to the ground to catch the direction of the moving herd gone over a ridge when the smoke came, but he could see no red point of light anywhere. He held himself motionless. It could be a meat camp or a war party or even a whole Kiowa or Comanche village, with scouts far out, enemies who might be within war club distance from him right now. If he had the time to hold himself still and unmoving half a night, as the warriors did, he might feel out the camp and the scout nests, avoid stumbling into them. There would be no danger from anyone except the scouts out moving in the unlucky nighttime, which was known to soften the moccasin with its dew, stretch the bowstring so it refused to send the arrow on its path.

But Elk couldn't wait, no matter how dangerous the night. If he let the horses get to water he would have to start the whole hopeless chase once more. Yet danger stood like a wall all around him, holding him from any move. He sharpened his ears like the listening fox and slowed his breath to test the night air for smoke again, trying to catch the direction of it, and of the sound and the living of the night. Cautiously he put his ear to the ground once more, but there seemed nothing under the sliver of waning moon except the swinging, purposeful walk of thirsty horses. Stiffly the young Indian drew himself together and took one silent step, then another, and finally he faded into the shadowy draws. When the smell of smoke seemed safely behind him, he began to run after the horses that were heading southwest by the stars and not stopping, no matter how weary the colts might be.

Elk was tired too, worn as a coyote that had been fleeing

13

all day before a prairie fire, but as the moon hazed in a thin clouding the hoofs ahead hurried faster, drawn by some far smell of water. Once more Elk had to run to scatter a cluster of dark shadows from a drying pond and do it without whoop or noise for enemy ears. But this time the herd did not start away, just watched a short distance off. Elk walked around the muddy bank to leave the disturbing man smell, yet the mares still tried to sneak in around him. He snatched the calico strips from his braids and tied them to rosebushes on the bank. But the horses still hung around in uneasy clots of darkness, always just out of reach of the Indian's rope, one trying to run around him on this side, one on the other, until he was driven to take the chance of a little fire. He threw together a narrow smudging row of twigs and leaves for a slow burning, one that would make little flame until he was well back in a dark draw if enemies were around.

Reluctantly the mares started their faltering colts away from the smell of smoke, and once more Elk had to start too, stiff and worn-out, when he could be home asleep. He could be deep in the soft bed robes instead of dozing as he ran over the dark, cactus-patched prairie, feeling ready to go down like a horse with a foot in a badger hole.

But the bear-marked colt drew Young Elk on, and he hoped that he was still following the right horses. Several times he heard what seemed to be fresher, wilder bunches, one with a whitish horse standing out plain in the dark of night, although this surely was not the white stallion from down in the Comanche country. It was said that a horse like that one could not be caught. Trapped, he would kill himself somehow: leap a cliff or break his neck right on level ground.

As Elk hurried to keep the horses moving, he tried to detect the small dragging steps of a young colt, yet any would be worn and sleepy now, so he could only follow

14

into the light of dawn. To keep himself awake as his worn moccasins felt out the rough ground, he began to talk softly to this Bear Colt, speaking the words to himself, as in a dreaming.

"Let me catch you, tame you, care well for you," he murmured in his coaxing, gentling way. "We will have a softness in our breasts for each other. I will warm to the sight of you on the hillsides, and you will come to my call, and if I am hurt you will not leave me, as I shall pursue anyone who steals you to the ends of the horizon. We shall harm no living thing, but together we shall be one, a tall man-horse, or, better, a horse-man, for there will be much more of you, Bear Colt, my brother, than of me."

As Young Elk plodded dully behind the stubborn herd, he realized that these were not proper words for the son of two great warrior families, not the dreams of coup-counting and scalp-taking expected of him. Yet he hardly expected to capture Bear Colt any more now, worn out as he was and sodden as an old cottonwood in the Arkansas River, his heavy moccasins lifting themselves without will or thought. The horses were wearing out too. Elk almost stumbled over a colt left behind, not breathing any more. He turned it up. There was no bear mark on it, no white mark of courage. Soon another colt was left in the grass, the mare driven on by the stallion with his angry, trumpeting call.

It was true that horses had less native endurance than man, were without the strength Young Elk got from his sparing gnaws at the pemmican and his swallows from the water bag, although the herd snatched grass here and there too, even a little water. If Elk could last —

When the warm dawn cleared, the young Cheyenne found himself close to Bear Colt, the old mare a good whooping distance behind the straggling herd. The stallion, weary too, let her go to the failing colt, stumbling, but still too fast for the worn Elk. Once he took his rope down, but, as though smelling the danger, the colt staggered on, growing stronger with the increasing day.

The sun rose and spread a shimmer of heat dance along the western horizon, crossed overhead, and still the young Indian plodded on, his legs really broken with fatigue, his feet bleeding from the cactus and brush and rock of the long chase. He was in strange country now, dry, gray, with little except snakes, lizards, and scrubby sagebrush. No sign of buffalo, not even an antelope running his curious semicircle, or a rabbit hopping. By midafternoon Elk was still following the slow dust of the horses, but more to be led out to water than to turn their direction or for any capturing. There was little weight left in the water pouch, and since yesterday he had been saving it for the suffering colt. For his own burning thirst he tried to work a pebble around in his mouth, but his stubborn tongue remained dry and swelling.

Then suddenly Young Elk had to realize that he was being trailed. Perhaps he had suspected it since he followed the faltering colt out on the bare, empty plain, with no draws, no snake-head gullies that might offer escape if enemies came. It was reckless, but the gaunted little foal had been going down every few steps, although still brave, springing up at every approach, still trying to overtake the old mare, to cling to her shriveled bag, surely dry of milk long ago. Worn as the colt seemed, and taming, Young Elk was stumbling too, with shimmering heat burning his back and his eyes, his feet swollen and awkward as stumps of wood.

There seemed no birds to fly up in warning, but Elk watched the sky for the eagle or the buzzard making a sudden turn. He finally saw something of the enemy himself — three Indians leading extra horses, coming along a far draw, very cautiously, perhaps unwilling to believe that

16

one youth could be out here alone, afoot. He must be a decoy, a bait for an ambush.

Young Elk could not run now, or even hope to hide. Besides, the colt was staggering and falling again, his legs crumpling, and this time Elk stood still and made his soft, gentling song in his parched throat. The gaunted colt clambered to his forelegs and then up, but instead of stumbling after the mare he turned and came toward the Elk, spraddle-legged, head down and swaying, the poor swollen tongue far out. He came to Elk as to one he had known a long time, as he had for two of his four days of life, his poor nose groping at the youth's clothing, trying to suck at the ragged shirttail. The young Indian laid his arm over the thin, bony neck and held the colt to him a moment, looking off the way the herd was straggling, knowing they must be following the smell of water somewhere in the breaks standing bluish against the southwest. But behind him and his colt were the stalking men, and although the sun was lowering fast, the enemy would be upon them before dark, and by then the colt might have died if he got no milk or even water. So Elk slipped his rope in a hackamore about the bony head and helped the colt into a little washout and dribbled the bit of water left in the skin pouch into his eager, uplifted mouth. Then he tied the sticks of legs together and laid the struggling colt out carefully so he could not get his back downhill. Even the strongest horse can die in a few hours that way, Elk knew. Afterward he looked carefully back over the empty plain before he slipped out to try to catch the loitering mare, plodding slowly after the rest now. He hurried almost to dropping and considered trying to halt her with an arrow, just to cripple her a little, but he could not get close enough for a sure shot with his little hunting bow and he would not wound her foolishly.

Then suddenly the three Indians were there, but ahead

17

of him, rising out of a canyon, riding for him across the sun-yellowed evening plain. Elk ran back toward the washout, for he must not let the Bear Colt die tied with a rope, die with his legs shamefully tied. It was a good white man's mile away, and only the thought of the colt got Elk there ahead of the whipping enemies. He fell into the hole with tearing breath and red streaks before his eyes. The colt was alive and kicking feebly. Young Elk dug in under the bank, hacking at the soft earth with his knife as his pursuers stopped short of the washout, apparently still fearing a trap. They kept back and shot arrows into the hole, Kiowa and Comanche war arrows, and Elk returned several of them to hold the men away while he pushed the leg-tied colt into the hole and then backed in too, as far as he could get.

By now the entire washout was in deep shadow, the arrow points glistening in the slanted sun as they came from both sides, and Elk knew that the warriors would certainly be in upon him with war clubs and knives before he could try to get away in the coming dusk. They would kill him, and then the colt, brave as the bear of courage on his side, would die, for no one would trouble with such a poor creature.

Angered by this thought Young Elk set another of the arrows sticking around him to the bowstring, and then another and another, arcing them to fall near the washout, shooting fast, trying to make it seem there were several warriors here. At least the men up there wouldn't get him with their arrows like a porcupine's risen quills sticking foolishly unused all around him.

One arrow surely hit, for a man roared out an angry word, an angry Cheyenne word. Apparently they knew Elk's tribe without seeing even one of his arrows. It seemed they crept up around him in earnest now, for the arrows came in straighter. He squeezed in tight against the colt, the poor little creature sucking at his braid, at the torn cloth of his shirt, at his ear. It was so pitiful that the young Indian wanted to leap out, defy these enemies with his naked knife, kill them all to save the poor little spotted horse.

Then he heard more words from the fading light above him, awkward Kiowa words for " Give up! " and something perhaps intended as the same in Comanche, and finally in clear Cheyenne. The sudden hope for Bear Colt made Young Elk reckless, made him forget that Cheyennes sometimes became part of the enemy both by capture and by marriage.

" I am Cheyenne! " the Elk called out. " Of the Cut-finger People! "

There was a silence as of whispering, and then a roar of laughter. " So you are a Cut-finger? More truly a crooked-tongue Kiowa son of a captive! Where is your party? "

" There is no party. I am alone — Young Elk, son of Elk River."

There was a snort of disbelief. " Elk River has then truly fathered a foolish one, to stray so far — "

" I was chasing a colt."

" Alone? Why should one not yet a warrior be permitted so far in enemy country? '

" It is our country too," Elk replied angrily, and immediately realized the danger of his hasty tongue. " It is true that the enemy — that others — are more often here," he had to admit in his fear for Bear Colt.

There was a mumbling in the dusk above to this, and finally one man crept nearer in the thickening dark before the moon's rise. He asked, and answered, many questions. He talked like a good Cheyenne, and because Young Elk had to get quick help for his colt he finally let himself be coaxed out into the light of a little fire that the men

19

shielded from the prairie with their blankets. He saw their faces, their accouterments. Plainly they were Cheyennes — three young men who had gone down southward afoot from Bent's Fort to locate some good horses, not mustangs, but the larger ones, the Spanish horses of the Texas settlements. They got away with some good ones from a Kiowa and Comanche camping but had to stand off a lot of arrows and finally run for it, losing their little herd. They sneaked back in the night and got a few very good horses, good enough to carry them away very fast, all dropped as they played out except the six left here.

"Our young friend is impatient with your long tongue," one of the men interrupted the speaker. "It seems he would say something."

Young Elk was hurt by the words that were spoken as of a boy, but he could not protest, not with the colt tied in the washout, perhaps already dead. They jumped down with a twist of burning sagebrush for light. The tough Bear Colt was alive, sucking at Elk's shirt as he untied the cramped legs. "It is this bear upon his side that I have been following," he tried to explain.

"The colt is a very poor and starving one to risk a life among enemies," the oldest of the Cheyennes said as he poured a little water over the blackened tongue and into the sucking mouth.

Young Elk made the sign of agreement as he drank sparingly and began to chew a little pemmican for the colt to suck, as he had heard could be done. And while he chewed he moved his weary hand over the white bear patch, rubbing the sand away slowly, and more slowly, until he was asleep, bent over the colt. The three Cheyennes squatting around the tiny coals laughed a little, but gently.

2

*Y*OUNG ELK came home very bad-faced, shamefaced that he had let himself be trapped in a washout deep in enemy country. That the captors down there turned out to be Cheyennes was undeserved good luck. He was reminded of this at the little council in the village circle the evening he returned. Only luck or some very strong medicine had kept him from being killed by the three who found him before they discovered what he was. That would have brought shameful ostracism upon three good men — for, as he knew, any Cheyenne who shed the blood of a tribesman must be driven out — or if Young Elk had been killed or captured by the Kiowas, Comanches, or even the Utes his people would have had to undertake a large avenging, one fitting the son of Elk River, the brother of a Bowstring society warrior, the nephew of Owl Friend, who had organized this soldier society. In return there would have been enemy revenge upon the Cheyennes, and so more avenging in return, on and on, with no telling how many would be dying for one foolish youth, how many helpless women and children killed too.

The smoke from the evening fires crept in long blue layers under the golden sun. It was the time for laughter and games, but Young Elk had to stand before his father and the other councilors, be shamed by their reminding words, words doubly shaming in the soft, flowing speech of the Cheyennes.

"I only wanted to catch Bear Colt," Elk said unhappily.

"No one has the right to forget the people. He must not endanger even himself if this can bring danger upon the rest," the father said sternly, and the youth held himself straight and unmoving, unblinking, as a just reproof demanded of a Cheyenne.

The others of the council circle looked up at him awhile over their guttering pipes and then beyond, to the loitering young men pretending not to be listening, and to the women who stopped a watching moment to see what would be meted out to Young Elk. Before these, their people, the headmen remained silent and firm, even against the women who were for a softening, and against the respectful demeanor of the youth who stood in the long silence before them.

Finally the old chief spoke: "Now it is enough from us."

But there was still the punishment from the Bowstrings, the warrior society that had been selected to police and guard the village all the past moon. No one could be permitted to slip out like this unpunished, and this time doubly punished because the Elk's brother was a member of the Bowstrings and his uncle the originator. Young Elk realized this, and knew that every dark eye in the village circle, Red Sleeve's too, surely Red Sleeve's, would be following his moccasin step as he walked slowly through the twilight to the big warrior lodge set up in the policing place. He hesitated and then scratched politely at the opening. To a call from inside, he stooped into the duskiness and glanced apprehensively around the circle of impassive, firelit faces, his own brother no more recognizing than the rest. No one asked Young Elk to sit, so he stood inside the opening, shrunken, like a boy. He did not dare

22

to lift his eyes again to the circle of men around the coals, so formal and strange here, with the official wolfskins of the society over their shoulders. Finally the war chief of the lodge, one of the bravest men of all the Cheyennes, looked up over the pipe at his lips. Slowly he began to speak, secret words with secret meanings, words that could never be repeated outside of the lodge door.

Young Elk was there a long, long time, but finally he was given his punishment, one he could never put to words either, nor even understand completely, as no one who was not a member of the society was ever to understand. It was true that the Elk received the usual sharp cuts of the bow of police authority across his gaunted back and shoulders. This much everyone knew, and was the easiest to bear. All of it was easier than the sorrow he knew sat in the eyes of his mother and his young sister, and in his second mother's too, as he passed them at the cooking fires. Running hard, he headed out to where Bear Colt lay flat and unstirring, his starved bones sharp as a birdling's under the thin skin. But the young foal still sucked at Elk's finger, and so he hurried to the family herd out in the darkened hills to fetch a mare in milk. He tied her with a close picket rope and a kicking hobble. Then, fighting her lusty colt away, he held up the Bear while he pulled weakly at a teat.

When the colt could find not one more drop for all his bunting, the Elk tied a skin bag over the mare's udder. "You'll have to learn to like grass a little faster now," he told her foal when he came pushing in, searching all over the skin cover, trying to suck it. Then Elk picketed the mare and settled down with Bear Colt, holding a palm on the sleeping head as he went over the things of this evening in his mind. Once he rubbed his welted shoulder where the punishing bows had struck.

The three men who caught him out on the prairie had been stern too, but good. Two of them had gone back immediately through the rising moonlight to a little water hole they had passed earlier, to shoot a buffalo cow and bring the milk-filled udder to the colt, help him suck it dry. So Bear Colt was kept alive all the way home, by milk from one cow after another. In addition the men came far off their trail with Elk, letting him ride one of their extra horses and carry the colt before him.

Of course Elk's father had given the men proper presents, and the mother opened the parfleches for beaded guest moccasins and took down bladders of pemmican to nourish their homeward way. Then they had started on, anxious to get home.

"You have a bold son," they told the father as he walked beside them to the edge of the village, as was proper. "The boy could have escaped us easily but he would not leave the colt — not with his legs tied, helpless."

"It is a worthless creature," the father apologized.

"One cannot truly say," the departing Cheyennes replied as they hurried on their trail.

The days passed slowly, and Bear Colt seemed to get no stronger. Young Elk kept his anxiety to himself, feeling hot and ashamed as he went about his village duties. There was no more criticism from his elders, as was good, but the younger boys teased him as he passed calling him Bone-catcher, one who drags home worthless bones that the wolves have gnawed and left. But there was another ridicule that was more difficult to bear — the taunting in the dark eyes of Red Sleeve as she passed along the evening water path where the young men of the village loafed, hoping for a gay word and a flirtatious glance. Yet Young Elk went and the maidens came walking out in their demure way with the waterskins, their hair neat, their everyday garments well fringed, their moccasins light. The young men were boisterous, happy, or anything that seemed to make them look like big men. Only Elk was silent, unnoticed. He even went to the early dances around one big fire or another. He endured fewer slights here, with the elders about. Although Red Sleeve only drew him into the whirling dance circle once an evening, for politeness, a few of the others remembered that Young Elk was of best family, handsome when not leaned down like the white man's greyhound, and usually with a gay tongue and flying feet to spin the others into laughing dizziness. But there seemed a new shyness in the maidens, so he took a double turn at the drumming and the songs now, and he did this well and freed his friends for the girls.

He also took his turn with the arrow-making, cutting and smoothing the shafts, gluing the feathers under the direction of the arrow maker. Much of the time he was out herding the village horses. He never liked to kill, but he worked hard during the buffalo surrounds at all the things that brought no demand for his bow. He helped to find and watch the herds, trying with careful, cautious use of distant man smell to hold them from leaving the country, from scattering too far, until the hunters could be in place and ready for a good charge from all sides with their arrows and spears. Afterward he helped the women and the boys and old men to skin and butcher, to pile the meat on the ready horses, and finally to bring the pack string into camp through the evening light. There Elk worked with the meat dividers so no kettle would be empty, carrying packs of fresh buffalo to this old couple or that woman without a hunter. The next day he helped with the drying racks and the hides to be tanned.

All this was good in the eyes of the Cheyennes, but it brought no glory around the evening fires when the exploits of the day were recounted. Two Wolves, his brother, had killed four fine, fat buffaloes. Another had dropped a lead cow that was getting away and taking much of the herd with her. What Elk did brought no warm looks of pride to his mother, to his young sister, White Moccasin, or to his second parents — no hidden pride to his father or his warrior brother, no notice from the young men, and none at all from Red Sleeve, high-headed and handsome as a young mustang on a fall hill.

The only one who might have honored the Elk was Old Horsecatcher, and all that the young Cheyenne had ever caught was the miserable Bear Colt. But in a month the foal was strong enough to follow the foster mother, sucking from one side while her own colt drew heavily at the other, with Young Elk watching that the mare did not kick. Gradually, too, the bird that rode the mare's back became friendly with Elk, barely flying away as he sprang up beside it to take the horses to better grass.

The teasing turned to others with newer sore spots to strike with the arrows of laughter. Besides, the camp was busy moving to clean ground up on the Platte. Although Young Elk always helped with the herd of his second father, Owl Friend, he spent much of his time with the family herd to be near Bear Colt. The moving was pleasant, the village large and with enough warriors to discourage attack. It was a slow and easy going. The four headmen led out, most of the way afoot, often sitting to smoke and to visit awhile so the people could rest. Behind them rode the head warriors, with a scattering of their men all around the moving camp, the scouts riding far out in every direction.

Inside this good wall of protection the people felt safe, first the young people on their horses, and closer in, where they were most protected, the women riding with their babies on their backs, or in the skin sacks hanging from the saddles, or in the pony drags that also carried the old and the sick and the bundles and rolled lodge skins.

Young Elk saw little of this from the herds, which were

kept back out of the village dust and stirring up their own. But once, while up with the others to eat in a shady spot, he overheard some of the men talking at their smoke.

"Your son is much like you in your raw years, Elk River, with his friendship for horses," one of the men told Elk's father.

"I remember when you risked your life in the ice-breaking of the Yellowstone to save a young colt. He was worth little, but he was caught on the little island, with the flooding ice grinding around his feet!"

An old man among them laughed, agreeing. "Ah-h-h, our Elk River! And everyone praised your courage and your pity for the little horse, and began to call you by our village name for the river, but I remember we had to make you stand before us for punishment."

"In that too, Young Elk is like the father — recklessly risking himself for a foolish little horse."

"But I put no danger upon the village," the father objected.

"Risking a valuable young warrior is a kind of danger too —"

Young Elk slipped away back to his horses, wondering how much of this was said for him to hear by these good men. He remembered the story, but this was the first time he heard it with the seeing heart.

When the village was well settled and fresh meat made, there was a bustle of preparation for a horse-taking expedition. It would be led by the wise and cunning Yellow Wolf, with a couple of other important men along, and eighteen warriors. They were going south to the upper Arkansas River for some good wild stock to build up the herds. Young Elk hung around the fringes of the planning, and once he even edged up to his father, ready to put his wish into words. But Elk River pointed out that only those

27

already famous at horse-trapping and raiding could hope to go with a man like Yellow Wolf. The Elk withdrew, and slipped in to the fire at his mother's lodge. He sat there very quietly, and she finally looked at him with concern in her gentle eyes but, knowing that it is not good for a mother to soften, to weaken, her son by sympathy, she held her silence.

Yellow Wolf's party left in darkness and camped at a far creek, so if they were seen by spies it would be harder to find their village for attack or, by its location and the direction the party was traveling, to plan an ambush. Late the first day out they noticed a lone rider, perhaps an enemy decoy, not far away. They stopped while some slipped around through a draw and surrounded the follower, only a youth, a Cheyenne youth — Young Elk.

"Ah-h-h! Truly a second time this foolish one would have been very easy to kill!" Yellow Wolf said angrily, curling his scornful lip even lower.

But, as Elk had hoped, they couldn't send him back alone now, and so he was taken along on condition that he keep silent and out of the way. This was work for experts.

Not daring to speak even one respectful word of gratitude, he made the sign of understanding. He was given the hard work, the mean tasks of the camp — water hauling, dressing the meat, moving the extra horses for grass. No one spoke to him except to command that this be done, or that. After the work of the catching began he was allowed to help keep the fast extra horses ready and to cut brush for the trap in a box canyon far below the Arkansas. He watched the men select and trap the herds, thirty-five in the first one, mostly fine young stock, many sorrels and bays and all very wild. He tried to see how everything was done, but mostly he was out with the men who guarded the horses already caught. The rawhide grazing hobbles

28

on their legs prevented running, escape, but they got tangled in brush and timber and made the horses easy prey for the plume-tailed prairie wolves or an occasional bear or mountain lion. Even Cheyennes from another village might pick up the horses if they were left unmarked and unguarded. But the great danger was from enemies come to sweep the herd away — the herd already fine enough to attract a large party, one with power to whip the Cheyennes. In addition to the value of the fine horses would be the humiliation of such a loss to a party under Yellow Wolf. Even a complete wiping out would not be impossible if the Cheyennes lost all their horses.

Three herders did nothing but watch for enemies, men with guns, good guns, while Long Bow, who knew the ways of winning a horse, put in his time taming the wild ones. He worked particularly with the best, and in this Young Elk's help was welcome, for his hand was a gentling one, and the black bird that lives with horses did not fly up to alarm the herd when he came near.

Finally one morning while Yellow Wolf and two others watched from a knoll, the warriors cut out the best of the horses and started homeward with them. Young Elk was left with the men holding the rest until the selected ones were safely gone, before they sent their herd flying off over the wild prairies again. It was while they were whooping these castoffs westward, to get the stallions far from the young mares Yellow Wolf was taking home, that Elk saw the golden horse. He came from the west somewhere and was suddenly standing on a ridge, his mane and tail gleaming like Zuñi silver. He looked curiously toward the dust and commotion, and after the mares of Yellow Wolf's herd. Long Bow whooped and flapped his blanket to scare him off. The horse was bold, but after a while he pivoted on his hind legs and was gone to join his own little herd,

29

waiting quietly far off, and then running.

"He was a fine one, that yellow stallion," Long Bow said afterward, when they rode to overtake the Wolf. "Fine, but nothing like the White One I saw down in the Comanche country a winter ago, the horse that no one will catch. He was like a mist animal, a white cloud horse standing on a hill with wind blowing his mane."

Young Elk saw the light in the old horse tamer's face and wished he could go to the Comanche country someday, when there was less danger, less war. If he were a warrior —

The Cheyennes pushed their new horses through two starlit nights, following the lead of Yellow Wolf and a companion, both men who knew the country and the ways of the enemies in it. Toward Black Lake they smelled buffalo chips burning and sent back a soft owl hoot of warning. The lake, just ahead, was so briny that only very thirsty buffaloes and water-starved horses came to drink, but not people. Beyond lay a spring of sweet water, and there the trails of buffaloes, mustangs, and pony drag poles too were very deep. Two scouts followed the smell of the burning chips to the spring. While one held their horses the other slipped afoot down the slopes that were dark with grazing herds to a wide scattering of fires, and heard Comanche talk all around him. When this news came back, a war bow was thrust into the hands of Young Elk and he was sent with the horse holders and the wild herd up beyond the spring. They moved the herd very slowly, cautiously, so no warning of noise and shake of earth could reach the Comanche camp.

"When you are safely past, stop until you hear yelling and firing. Then start the herd homeward with whoop and blanket," Yellow Wolf had said.

For once Young Elk did not want to beg to go with the leader, even if it could be done. Quietly he helped to hold the more restless of the mustangs with his soft murmurings as they started to edge outward for a break to the open night prairie — even the leaders hampered with walking clogs on their legs tried it. The guards knew that Yellow Wolf and the warriors were close to the Comanche camp waiting for the first paling of day. Walking Coyote, a bold young man on the fastest horse, was selected to stay behind after the raid to hold the pursuit back while the rest got away. It was a very great honor and a dangerous one, but if he lived the exploit would be told at all the campfires, and pretty girls would draw close, soft-eyed, murmuring their admiration.

Before dawn Yellow Wolf changed his plans a little. He sent a messenger to order the herd moved on farther and when the man went back he took Young Elk along. The Elk asked no questions, but once he said, " I do not wish to kill anybody."

" You are to slip in among some horses, with your quieting hand — " the man whispered, and in this Elk was pleased, but made uneasy again when a war ax was slipped into his belt. They had located a fine little herd, the man said, but it was very well watched, the horses fast ones and nervous, restless. Young Elk, slighter than a warrior and with no sign of the warrior about him if he were seen in the darkness, might be useful in this.

With a foreboding and an excitement that he had never felt before, the Elk left his horse with the holders in a draw and crept off in the dark direction that the messenger pointed. It was a soft, still night, the horses moving all the time, perhaps from the mosquitoes, bad even up on the high ridge. Elk came in, slowly from downwind, stooping low, starting and stopping much as a wandering colt might, until he was among the horses. Several shied a little from him, but they were not more restless than before. They did not waken the herders; they had not slept, not even with the lead mares hobbled so they could not stampede and draw the herd away. It was these hobbles the Elk was to cut and, while he was locating them, he must select a fast mare and wait for dawn and the attack on the other herds. Then he was to mount and start the horses away, to meet the others at a little creek when the sun was climbing above the shoulder. There they would wait a while for anyone missing to come in, at least a while.

Every time the herders rode near Elk's hiding place his heart pounded and his hand crept to the ax at his waist, but he kept himself still as a sleeping colt curled up on the ground. When a whiteness began to climb out of the east he moved stealthily, cutting the hobbles of one mare after another, but there was no one to tell him that the fast-looking one was a snorter. At her first warning, the herders came riding, apparently knowing there was a man among the stock. Elk squatted still, hoping the other horses wouldn't scare at the mare's faunching and noise, run over him. Then, just as it seemed the herders must discover the cut hobbles and Elk, still crouched on the ground, there was a far whooping, with gunshots off in the other herds and shooting from the village, all at once. The restless horses around Elk bolted southward. All he could do now was grab the mare's tail as she started. He was jerked along behind her in great flying steps until he managed to lengthen his jumps and the rhythm of them to carry him up on the rump of the mare, clinging to her flanks, pushing himself forward with hands and toes until he could get a hold in the flying mane. A bullet and some arrows whistled past him, but he clung tight.

The Elk rode close to his horse, plainly a good war mare, trained to carry off any stranded or the wounded, no matter how they fastened themselves to her. He kept to the far side from the shooting as much as he could, thinking only of getting away with the horses, even though they were headed in the wrong direction. But the herders had light to see now, and twice their arrows and a bullet too struck the mare, and yet she kept running, but her breath was a gurgling whistle, so Elk knew she was bad hit and grieved that such a good horse must die for his coming.

But the young Indian had to think about the Comanches whipping hard after him, while another one was cutting in from the side, trying to head the horses, turn them back to the village and their warriors. Then Elk's mare stumbled and he knew he must act fast. The first time a horse came close in the breakneck run, he grabbed at the streaming mane and leaped for the back, but the animal swerved in fright and left Elk to bang and pound at the laboring ribs. Yet he managed to hang on until he got a good flying kick at the ground with a moccasin toe, enough to swing him up on the stampeding horse that was running down at the earth in his terror, low like a coyote fleeing for his life, but breathing hard, a soft stallion, although a good gray color, but fat and soft.

Elk thought of the Comanche guns and of prairie dog holes, but without a jaw rope he couldn't control this untrained horse and would just have to hang on until the stampede ran out. Once he looked around for the Comanches, but he was near the tail end of the herd, in such a thick cloud of dust that he couldn't see anything. Yet with the lead mares swinging far to the right, the Comanches could cut across, bring the Elk down. He was alone and far from help. He must keep the herd running straight on, but that would take a faster horse, one to overtake the lead mare.

He looked ahead into the dust and, seeing how far behind he was, he managed to pound the head of his horse sideways and cut across the herd himself. But before the lead mare saw him coming, some Comanches struck in, whooping. She swerved from them and turned the herd eastward, leaving several horses lost in the thick dust. A big brown-bay near the lead saw the turning a little late and came running to overtake the slower ones, including Elk's horse. She ran head up, like a fleeing wild one, but not entirely wild, for when Elk whistled the warrior's call, she turned in alongside and he left his slow horse for her back. The next time he looked around for the Comanches he realized perhaps why Yellow Wolf was so anxious to get this little herd. Even the slow stallion Elk had just left seemed to be lengthening the string of dust he kicked into the pursuers' eyes.

Most of the best Comanche stock had been picketed beside the owners' lodges for safety and readiness if there was an attack. Walking Coyote had singled out a very fine bay tied at a chief's lodge and waited ready for daylight, the time for changing herders. At Yellow Wolf's signal the Cheyennes charged into the unguarded herds, yelling, waving their blankets, stampeding the horses to the north. The herders whipped back out, firing their few guns, but they were too far away and too surprised to hit anybody.

In the camp the warriors poured from the lodges at the first whoop, but many of their horses jerked their pickets free in the excitement and followed the stampeding herds. Walking Coyote got clear into the village, jumped off his horse, cut the big bay loose and was mounted and gone before anyone could send even an arrow after him. He caught up with Yellow Wolf and handed him the rope of the bay. Then the Coyote and a few others who had guns dropped back to hold off the pursuers. It was hard in the running and dust for the raiders to tell which were escaping camp horses running to join the stampeding herds or had Comanches hanging to the far side. Everybody had to keep dodging the flying picket pins in the boiling dust and the warriors of both sides shooting. One Cheyenne was wounded and two Comanches were killed, yet they kept coming until they saw the wild herd of the Cheyennes. So many strange horses must have carried a great war party somewhere in ambush. Besides, there was another big dust coming in from the southeast. In the face of this double danger the last of the Comanche pursuers turned and fled for their camp, leaving the Cheyennes laughing at their going, shouting, motioning their taunts. The big flying dust had only one Cheyenne in it — Young Elk, whooping the herd along, kicking the weary flanks of his horse at every jump.

There was praise for the Elk, and disappointment in him too. He had saved most of the herd of fine southern horses, but the stallion that Yellow Wolf wanted particularly was lost, left behind. For hunting and war, mares were better, quieter, with more endurance, mares and geldings. The fine big gray stallion Wolf wanted for breeding was soft, too soft for the long run. He had played out and was lost in the dust perhaps where the herd turned from the Comanche pursuers.

Several of the warriors backtracked with Young Elk but, as he expected, in a half day's ride they couldn't find the stallion. He was gone, picked up by the Comanches or plodded back home by himself. Elk was very humiliated by this. He should have realized Yellow Wolf's plans, known even without any words said that the big soft gray he left for the faster mare was the one the leader wanted.

The expedition was a lucky one so far, and after a day's rest and care for the wounded in a well-guarded canyon, they started home. But they struck the trail of about thirty lodges going north with very many horses along, perhaps Kiowas, those traders of the Plains, taking the horses to the Crows to get elk teeth, ermine skins, and other northern luxuries. There was more sign of what looked like a little Cheyenne war party stalking the Kiowas, hoping to sweep away a few horses perhaps, or pick up a scalp or two to avenge some deaths last spring.

Yellow Wolf overtook the little party of tribesmen with some of his warriors while the rest held the horses. Together the Cheyennes charged out of the misty dawn hours upon the moving Kiowa camp. They fled, and in the chase a woman who fell from her horse was overtaken. One man counted coup on her, touching her with his lance but making only a small flesh wound. She stopped her running and begged for her life, offering him the two-year-old child on her back, a little white girl captured in the south last spring. The Cheyenne had lost his little girl from a sickness, and he motioned the woman on and carried the blue-eyed child home. She rode in a skin sack at his saddle, or astride before him, laughing at all the men who brought her presents — pretty flowers, a shining stone, a tiny water snake to curl up so cunningly in her palm.

The Yellow Wolf party arrived at the Platte with great formality. Mirror signals told of their successful return from far out, and a welcoming escort came to bring them in. The great herd of fine horses, wild and Comanche, was driven past the village, strung out in single file so all could see the splendid catch. There were cries of admiration, and some louder cries of joy too, as this or that horse was recognized as one stolen from the Cheyennes in a Comanche raid last year. All these were restored to the owners, and the rest were divided among the raiders. For a week there would be trading of horses and racing and betting, and much present-making too, to friends and the needy.

No one in the village was happier than the woman with her little white girl, laughing and less shy than Indian children. Almost at once she slipped from the foster mother's arms to play with the little Cheyennes as with old friends.

Although there were no scalps or coups to count for

36

Young Elk at the evening fire, he was given the same share of horses as the other youths along, and in addition a fast young mare from the wild ones that he had already trained to lie down at a pull on the rope or the mane. This one Elk gave to his brother, a present that even a Bowstring warrior could appreciate. Two young grays went to Elk's father's herd and a fine young mare to the lodge of his second father and mother, as was the duty of every Cheyenne boy toward those who welcomed him as a son too. They could show him more open affection without keeping him a cradleboard youngling, without the woman making a little "second husband" of him, as happened in closeness with the blood, the nursing, mother and so without making him an enemy of his blood father.

Elk had a horse for his sister too, a pretty spotted yearling, and White Moccasin spoke her thanks in modest looking down. "Father, say to our brother that I am very proud."

Elk replied through the father too, for no Cheyenne boy could ever address his mother or his sister directly after he passed the seventh year. "It will please me to gentle the spotted horse to match the maidenly gentleness of our sister," he said.

Finally Young Elk took a strong, reliable mare with the marks of the Comanche pony drags to an old woman who had lost the only man of her family to a wounded buffalo. He tied the horse to the lodge and slipped away as the woman came stooping out the opening, exclaiming in happy disbelief. Elk still had two new horses left, good ones that he hoped someday to tie outside the lodge of Red Sleeve. Today the girl was smiling, but upon the young men who killed the Comanches, yet Elk was determined that it would not always be so.

While the others went from the victory dance to feast after feast, Young Elk slipped out to the moonlit herd, and when he whistled, Bear Colt did not come at once but stood off awhile, and so strong had he grown that he gave Elk a good tussle in the dark before he finally lay on the grass to be rubbed as he was the night he was first caught. But the soft Cheyenne words Elk made for the colt were for another too, for a golden yellow horse with mane and tail like Zuñi silver in the far sun.

3

*Y*OUNG ELK had come come home happy from the horse-catching. It was true he had been permitted to go along only because it was dangerous to send him back alone. Yet he had not angered the important men seriously, or interfered with the work, and he had seen much of horse-taking and -taming. Now he had to listen to his father's quiet complaint against his humiliating conduct.

"The son of great warrior peoples must not be like a homeless dog, sneaking in anywhere he can with visiting chieftains or the wood gatherers of evening —"

Afterward Yellow Wolf came privately to sit in the father's lodge. When the pipes were going well, the fragrance of sweet willow bark rising through the smoke hole, the Wolf spoke. "Your younger son shames us all with his coming where he has not been asked."

He said it with a humorous curl to his lip. Yet the truth lay so heavy in his words that Elk River could not laugh them out of the smoke hole, and the mother had to clap her hand to her mouth in mortification. In the long silence Yellow Wolf held his pipe in his hand, letting the glow of it cool. Finally he placed the stem to his weathered lips and relighted the bowl with a bit of fire.

"Your son is a Works-Well-with-Horses, like the early

men who first brought these new big-dogs-that-one-could-ride to us," he said, laughing a little to comfort the concern he saw in the face of his old friend.

"He is like the pemmican before it has found its shape in the carrying bladder. Unformed," Elk River replied soberly. "He has made his fasting and the dreams but it was not clear to anyone what the dreaming meant. Not even a good second father like Owl has helped in this. His brother, Two Wolves, has grown strong there, as have those given to our lodge as second sons."

"That is true; they are all good men. Your Two Wolves has become a fine young warrior with Owl —"

The father made the proper humble words. "New wood is soft for the bending, soft and green," he said. "Warrior sap flowed in all these. But it is the same with Elk, and yet he has no taste for war at all, no more than a girl; less. We have long had our warrior women, as you know, even here, and in our family there are women better hunters than our son."

"I have remembered this last moon that sometimes killing is not good for one like the Elk," Yellow Wolf admitted. "Yet if his belly becomes lean enough he will kill to eat. He will kill to live, even kill a man if that must be. I hear that he sent arrows back to the capturing Cheyennes from the washout when he thought they were enemies."

"He only scratched one, to keep them back. He was very close and could have done much more."

Yellow Wolf looked into the handful of fire coals a long time. "Perhaps another dream will come," he told the parents when he left, but his voice was not convincing.

Elk River spoke sadly of the Wolf's visit to his young son. The youth's reply was a difficult one to make but he felt it must be done. "I find no need for the fast or its dreaming. I have no love in my heart for these ceremonials."

Because no Cheyenne could be told what must be done, except to walk in honor, no more was said of this to Elk. Yet it was a time of blaming upon him, and he went more and more to the horses, particularly the new wild ones and Bear Colt and the foster mare with the black bird that rode her back and did not cry out in alarm when the Elk approached.

Often, too, the young Cheyenne's mind turned to the fine golden horse with the silver mane and tail that they had seen on the ridge far to the south, looking there toward the men while his little herd ran swiftly toward broken country, keeping close together.

The village moved southward for new grass, needed often with the Cheyenne horses as many as the stars of the night. Besides, the women wanted a clean place to live, new patches of wild fruit and a little visiting with other Cheyenne bands. Young Elk took his turn watching the village herds, idling the time away making a stiffened rawhide rope to catch the fine golden horse he had seen in the south, a chief's golden ceremonial horse. That other southern horse that men talked about, the White One, white as a great summer cloud rising over a hill — that one, Elk knew, was not for the rope or the gentling hand.

With his little hunting bow handy for rabbit or grouse, which he somehow never saw, or as a small threat against raiders, Young Elk liked to sit the nooning hour away high on a hill where he could look over all the surrounding country and down upon the herds scattered grazing along the slopes below him, working back from water. Beyond a low ridge, half a white-man mile away, were the new-painted skin lodges of the village. Elk couldn't see them, but he knew that the women and children were working under the trees or at the clear water of the creek, perhaps a few digging the prairie turnips on higher ground, while along the bottoms across the creek the boys and young men were racing in a game, their shouts and laughing carried to him in thin bits of sound on the wind. There would be the voices of the girls too, their songs for this one or that to win, his sister perhaps there, and surely Red Sleeve among them.

It was a still day, the grass so seedy and good that the horses did not wander much. Elk's riding mare was picketed near, handy for emergencies, mostly to drive off an occasional little bunch of watering mustangs that might toll the wilder young stock away. Most of the warriors, his brother too, were out in little parties, keeping enemies from moving too deep into the Cheyenne hunting grounds, and to count a few coups for honor in the village and in the soldier societies and perhaps toward a wife.

But there were many scouts out in all directions to avoid surprise of the village, and so Young Elk hummed to himself and to the little bird that sat on his horse while he braided at the rope and thought of the golden stallion.

Suddenly the bird flew up in a sharp crying. Young Elk laughed. "You don't think my song is good?" he started to ask, but the mare was looking off south, ears erect. Elk looked too and saw something moving along a shallow draw that led down between the horses and the village. He saw just the barest tops of heads, some with a feather — at least ten mounted men, perhaps more, cutting the horses and Elk too off from the village.

He sprang to his horse, yipped, and swung his bow to start the herd for the village. There was a Kiowa charge from the draw, some after him, swinging guns but not yet giving the village the warning that shots would be. The rest raced to head off the horses scattering in a run down along the slopes, trying to sweep away the Cheyenne herds. Elk slid down the side of his running mare, clinging by mane and toe hold over the galloping back as he set an arrow, but instead of firing it futilely against the enemy he sent it lightly into the fat rump of a lagging old mare before him. She leaped forward into the flying dust of the herds, sending them all into a thundering stampede toward the village as scouts from far out came whipping in too, but very far away, Elk knew, too far away.

When the first horses rounded the ridge people were running among the lodges, men cutting their picket horses loose and charging out to meet the enemy. But the Kiowas were drawing in upon the horses now, firing at Elk, the bullets cutting the air all around him, one striking his mare a little. Clinging as well as he could to his frightened, bullet-stung horse, Elk set arrow after arrow to the string, tearing back and forth between the attackers and the flying herd, trying to keep the Kiowas off a little longer, knowing only that the women and children must have these horses to get away if this was a big attack.

Then he saw the Indians charge upon a woman out alone digging turnips on a knoll. Through the dust he caught a glimpse of her running fall and a Kiowa riding over her. Angrily Young Elk turned his mare, his bow up just in time to send an arrow against a man who was swinging a war club for his head. The Kiowa's face flattened as the arrow struck. His legs let go and he slipped to the ground, the horses of the two men behind leaping him and coming on. One after the other tried to get the Cheyenne clinging to the dodging, flying mare. Finally one managed to knock Elk from the side of his horse, and as he went under the thundering hoofs he heard a Cheyenne war whoop, roaring and powerful, as though all the absent warriors were back in time for the fight.

Young Elk awoke to a dark cave of pain while somewhere, apparently outside of himself, there was a hot throbbing as of a spear point thrust again and again into flesh. It was a spear burning and hot for the shaping hammer, and something blazed before Elk's face too, something he could not escape, until gradually he realized that

43

this blazing was a nest of coals — a lodge fire — and the pain and burning were in his head, all in his throbbing head.

"He returns from the dying," a voice said softly. Elk recognized it — Ridge Tree, the medicine man — and the other Indian squatting beside him was his father. When Elk tried to move, Tree's wife held out a big horn spoon and the father fed his son soup from it in little sips over the edge.

"You have become a warrior," Elk River said quietly, holding his voice out of any pridefulness. "You held the enemy back until we could come up, and you have killed a man. Today you have become a warrior and your ceremonial name shall be Kiowa Killer."

Slowly Young Elk let himself back upon the soft robes, holding to his head that was whirling like a dust dance on the prairie, but after he was very sick it cleared away and even the grass bits the whirlwind had set to flying in his mind settled, leaving him empty and spent. A long time he lay there in his cave of pain, afraid to move, to waken the sickness again, and the throbbing in his head, in every joint. And gradually another, a deeper pain entered, the load of meaning in his father's words. He had killed; he, Young Elk, had killed a man.

But perhaps the words of his father, too, would be gone like the flying grass of the whirlwind.

The next few days Young Elk gradually lost the pain in his head and the shaking in his belly, but now he had to remember something of what had happened. He was told that the Kiowas had been chased clear south to the Smoky Hill River, and two more of them killed before the Cheyennes got tired and came home. The raiders got no horses, but one of Elk River's was shot and another broke a leg in the wild chase down the slope to the village. Oh, Bear Colt was safe, got left far behind in the wild run.

44

The woman struck down by the Kiowa was recovering too, and when the Elk was able to go about the village in his old way, it was fine to feel the eyes following him in warmth and approval, to overhear words of praise as for a young man truly become a warrior. Even so there was still a shadow over Elk's heart, like the thin gray clouding before the winter's storm. Then, at the moon's turn, the father made the naming feast for the Elk, with Two Wolves home from a fight with the Utes, and happy to help in the honoring of his brother. At the dance after the ceremony Red Sleeve drew Elk into the circle with her, not in politeness but flirtatiously, with soft eyes in the firelight. And yesterday she had stood in the fold of his blanket a few moments for a friendly word. It was the first time she had done this, although several times in the spring Elk had waited outside of her lodge with other young men. But she had always let him stand as she passed, laughing to the old woman of her lodge who walked just behind the girl, as was proper. Sometimes Red Sleeve went to visit friends, or even to stand for a moment in the blanket of another waiting one, always some youth already big in a warrior society.

But now Young Elk had saved the village horses, stood off a Kiowa charge all alone with nothing but a rabbit bow, and killed a seasoned warrior. So Red Sleeve drew him into the dance beside her a second time. As he was caught up in the flying circle to the drums and the singing, her hand was small and alive as a bird in his. Afterward she let him walk with her in the group that went toward her end of the village.

When the camp was dark and only a faint red of the coals glowed through the lodge skins, the Elk went out upon the chilly night prairie and lay with his face in the grass, his breast full of such a turmoil and sweetness that he knew tomorrow he must paint the color of it upon himself for all to see.

4

*Y*OUNG ELK awoke to the midday and looked about him as in a strange country, one very different from the place he had seen only a moment ago, a very green and misty place, with very, very many horses. He raised himself and finally stood up, weak and thirsting. It was true — the whole wide sweep of river valley was empty, with not one horse, no sign of a village or even of an antelope or bird. It was as though he had returned from a great and wearying journey into a desert land, or that all things had died while he was away.

But then he remembered that he had been in a dreaming, made because he must know what to do about the Kiowa he brought to the ground, when he was so firmly certain that he must not kill.

Now he had awakened on a bare gravelly ridge with no sign of his dream around him — nothing but a little sliver of the black glass from the steaming water country of the Yellowstone, the Elk River, and beside it a wing feather of the bird that lives with horses. Elk saw these with wonder and surprise. Carefully he placed them in the little pouch made for his medicine, his holy things, but empty all this long time.

Slowly the lean, gaunted youth managed to walk down

the slope to the river and dropped to the sandy bank, far enough from the water so a faint would not make him fall face-down into it, to drown. Holding himself back as he would a water-wild horse, he scooped up a palmful, but at the first swallow his belly sickened; later he drank a little more, and finally he built a fire to roast the thick stems of the arrowhead plant and made a curing tea of sweetroot and water in his rawhide belt pouch by dropping a hot stone into it for a little while.

Slowly Elk strengthened enough to make his purifying bath, and then lay in his breechclout under a tree to throw his mind back over the four days just past. He knew he should have told that he had gone out to make a fast, but with everyone so happy that he was a warrior he found it difficult to say how disturbed he was, even to his second father, the Owl, least of all to that great old war leader, the organizer of the Bowstring warrior society. So Elk had gone away alone, but he ran into his sister out training the yearling he had given her. He felt her wondering eyes following his moccasins as he passed, and so he returned and put a hand upon the back of the young horse and spoke earnestly. " My friend," he had said, " you will tell our sister that one may be gone the four days — " meaning the time of a fast.

Slowly now, as Elk lay on the riverbank, the four days since he said that came back to him. The second and third had been hard, with only the little night rain for water, but enough to chill his nakedness to shaking. Then the last day his dreaming came. It seemed that he was in some great danger, even as great as when the Kiowa struck him down in the horse raid. He was surrounded in what seemed a great storm of vague forms, enemy forms, sending bullet and arrow and lance against him, and when it seemed he must go under in this hailing, he heard a bird sing. It was the little black bird that lives with horses, the one that rides on the withers high above everything that happens, and sees how it all is.

But this time the bird was singing in words the Cheyenne could understand: "Work with horses and I will protect you," he sang, making it loud and sweet over all the noise of the bullets. "Become one with the horses but kill nothing except to live. Do this and you will be a strong one in the hearts of the evening fires."

Then Elk looked around and saw that now he was surrounded by running horses, wild ones with flying manes and tails, their nostrils flaring wide, foam-flecked, their eyes great and burning with the fire of the sun.

They were so thick around him no enemy could get through, and when a particularly fine one came past, Elk heard himself cry out in admiration: "You! You are the one —" and suddenly he was up on the horse, with the bird on the withers before him, riding together in the flying stream of beautiful horses, the bay and sorrel and black and gray, the spotted and the yellow, their manes flowing together, light and golden and twisting together like some wind-carried mist at sunrise. And when he looked down he was riding a great white horse, white as the mist, white as a cloud rising above a hill.

Even with the dreaming still upon him, Young Elk knew he must go home, stop the worrying of his people. Besides, the emptiness of the valley made him uneasy, and when he rounded the bend, the place where the village had been was empty, bare, the earth worn naked by hoof and moccasin, the fire spots dark, the ashes blowing a little. An old buffalo skull lay where his father's lodge had been, with knife scratches on the bleached forehead saying: "Gone south. Two sleeps," and in a box elder, safe from wild creatures, hung a little bladder of pemmican twisting lightly on its thin whang cord.

Young Elk cut off a chunk to gnaw and started along the village trail. He was still weak from the fasting and the thirst, but he would strengthen, strengthen in all but understanding. Who could tell him what this dreaming meant?

At the new camp Young Elk went straight to the lodge of Owl Friend. There his second mother fed him, scolded him a little in her outspoken, humorous way, and brought him the new moccasins due a returned dreamer. Elk took them to the creek nearby, soaked his swollen feet, dug out the cactus thorns, and went fittingly shod to his father's lodge. He went shamefaced, admitting that he should have said where he was going and made the proper rituals for the dreams out on the prairie. He knew it was foolish to do this improperly, and dangerous to go out alone with enemies skulking near, and exposing not only himself but the honor of the village. Although his sister realized that Elk could not have known of the sudden decision to move to new buffalo ground, she had to let the others think he had gone for more horses. Elk remembered how it was when Yellow Wolf came to Elk River because his son had sneaked out after the horse expedition like a homeless dog. Then Elk had realized how childishly thoughtless he had been, and that a man must measure all his actions so they do not bring humiliation upon others. But somehow it had been forgotten —

Now Elk River listened to the tall, arrow-thin son standing before him, and finally motioned Elk toward his empty place at the fire. Guttering his pipe thoughtfully, the father asked, " Did a dream come to you? "

At first Young Elk sat silent, knowing that while they were looking down upon the same thing, it was from opposite hills. His puberty fasting had brought only one little dream, plainly a foolish one, the men had all thought. He had seen a colt on a hill smelling the first snow, pawing in resentment, snorting, turning to run, and then circling back, once more accosting this unknown thing that the snow of winter was.

The old ones had talked a long time about the dream, some saying this, some that, but to all it seemed only a boy's night dreaming, without message. Not a vision.

"No," the boyish Elk had admitted softly then. He had barely managed to say that the colt had seemed to taunt him, his eyes burning with such a fire that it seemed he didn't see the boy at all and yet was looking at him.

The men had shook their heads to this. "Elk has horses on his mind now," one said. "But who can tell how it will be? He has a good eye for the arrow and the gun of his father."

"Ah-h-h, he is also a good dancer," Ridge Tree, the medicine man, reminded them that day. "He can make those who watch him see themselves as part of the Great Powers. Perhaps he might become a medicine dancer, one to lift the heart in time of trouble."

But Owl, his second father, would not have him lose any honors. "Perhaps Elk will still become a good warrior like the people of his father and mother," he said. "Let us wait."

Elk remembered listening to these words like the clouds of different directions. Looking down upon his crossed knees he had been ashamed that he was failing them all, but he hoped he had seemed attentive to their words as a good Cheyenne, attentive to all that was not the teasing.

But that was long ago, and now Elk was at his father's fire after a third slipping away in one summer. True, this time was for a second dreaming, but as he waited for words to come to him, Elk thought of Bear Colt and how his hair would feel under the hand, smooth and strong on the neck, soft as moleskin on the nose.

50

"Tell me what you saw," Elk River said at last, and with his pipe cooling he listened to a few words and then took his son to the lodge of Owl Friend. There, before several of the wise ones of the village, the youth told the dream, and when he was done they asked a few questions, his father and Owl too, and he heard the sadness in their voices when they finally said he must be tired from the hard trial and the long walk since.

"Sleep, and perhaps the sun will bring us all wisdom," Ridge Tree said.

In the morning Young Elk was taken to the sweat lodge. He had gone there before, not for ceremonials, for which he had no fondness, but to sweat out the pain of sprains, of weariness, or of sickness. Now he went for purification, and when he came out he dressed in clean buckskin and his new beaded moccasins. His hair was neatly braided, the little sliver of black glass from the hill of his dreaming tied over his ear with the feather of the bird that lives with horses.

In the meantime Elk River had gone with a gift robe to the Horsecatcher's lodge and smoked a slow, quiet time with the old man. At first the Catcher murmured against the father's plan. The boy was bold and brave; he should become a great warrior as his people were before him. There were many honors for the son of such warrior families —

"My son wishes only to catch horses," the father said sorrowfully, "and now it seems that the only vision he has been given, the only medicine, leads to that."

"In such a choice it is more than wishes, sometime more even than strong medicine," Old Horsecatcher replied, looking into the handful of coals. "How will it be for our son when the other young men are sung into the village for their coups against the enemy, and when the women make all their trilling cries of admiration for them,

51

while the Elk must ride in unwelcomed and unseen? How will it be later, when others, his own brother too, step into your place and Owl Friend's and those of the other honored men of his people? They will become the big men in the warrior lodges, the council, and in the tribe. That day will our young man be content with what horses have brought him?"

A long time these words hung like smoke in the lodge, smoke that would not let go. But finally the matter was done. Young Elk, waiting beside his mother's fire, watched out of the corner of his downcast eye. He saw his father come stooping from Horsecatcher's lodge and knew from the slow, firm step of his walk what the decision had been. Suddenly the youth was overcome by embarrassment and slipped away and out the back of the village. Fastening his rope about his waist he ran for the horses and rode off into a dusky draw.

At dawn he was near a spring he had seen when he hunted Bear Colt. He settled down to rest a little and to wait for the wild horses that might come in. The first herd had a fine young two-year-old stallion who looked back over his withers at Elk as the leader took them in a wide run around the spring, uneasy at the smell of man. Then suddenly Young Elk saw one of the birds whose feather he wore in his hair, and he had to remember his father and his errand to Horsecatcher. The honored council chief, Elk River, had gone to an old man for help for his son, and the son had run away foolish as a child fresh from the cradleboard.

Slowly the Elk went to his horse and rode home.

In the lodge the father looked a long time upon the son, his face stony as the canyon walls of the stream the Cheyennes call Elk River. Then without a word he motioned his long, strong hand toward the lodge of Horsecatcher. "Go!" he commanded, and this time Elk had to go, and alone, although it was surely a harder thing than the ordeal of the thongs through the breast at sun-dance time.

"I am foolish, and changing as the wind," he managed to say to the famous man. "You can make nothing of such a one."

A long time Horsecatcher bent over his pipe, the old face withered and remote in the red glow of the coals, giving no sign for the youth stooped in the lodge door. One bony old hand was stroking the little medicine bag that hung from the gray braids, the eyes lost in their nests of wrinkles or perhaps closed upon some private concern. And when it seemed that Young Elk must back out and take his shameful, unwanted carcass away, the old man spoke.

"Go rope antelope," he said.

"Run them?" Elk asked doubtfully. "Is it not better to make the pits? The antelope are very fast."

"Good that they are fast. Perhaps your brother will help you. He will cut in *so* and *so*," the old man said, his long, thin hand making sunfish motions. "When you have done this, return to me."

They went out early, Elk and the young warrior who would surely be as famous as his father and Owl Friend. Two Wolves was a lithe young man, fleet-footed, and yet a powerful wrestler. "Antelope?" he had asked when Young Elk carried the Horsecatcher's verdict to him. "Pick your fastest horse and bring the new rope you made."

Each led a running horse as they rode out beyond the prairie-dog towns with their thousands of busy little burrows that were such dangerous traps for hoofs in a hot chase. In a patch of sandy hills they flushed three antelope and singled out the young buck. After a short run the buck left their riding horses behind, and so they changed to the fast ones. By then he had circled around in curiosity, and Wolf started after him, motioning the Elk to the side. So they took turns cutting in on him from one side or the other until, toward noon, they got close. Elk took his rope down, whipped his horse into a dead run, and swung his loop just as the horse hit a hole and went down, with Elk going off over his head but striking the ground curled to roll. He stretched out slowly, feeling for broken bones, shook his aching body, and got up, but his horse was finished, a foreleg snapped off above the hock, the bone sticking white through the bloody hide. It was like a friend hurt to Elk, and so Two Wolves had to kill the horse with a knife to the throat. With Elk up behind Wolf, they went back to their riding horses, hidden in a draw, and then home.

Three days in succession they ran antelope and got advice each evening. Then Elk borrowed a very fast smoke-roan and started an antelope slowly, letting him do the running for several hours. Suddenly the youth let the racing smoke-roan go. With his ears laid back, his belly close to the ground, and his tail straight out, he started to overtake the antelope.

It was a one-man chase, and when Elk got close the antelope began to dodge like a rabbit, this way and that, but the horse kept just to the side and a little behind, until he saw the rope sing out. Then the roan sat back and the antelope went into the air, turned end for end, and hit the ground.

With running hobbles on him, and two ropes, one to each side and held by the riders so the animal wouldn't break his delicate legs, they brought the antelope in, fighting them all the way. Elk kept him with the horse herd. In a week there were two more, and Elk took them all to Horsecatcher's lodge and tied them to his picket pins. When the old man came out to look at the frightened, shivering antelope, all three fine, grown bucks, Two Wolves told the story of their capture so Elk need not seem immodest.

Horsecatcher listened and looked into the proud, hopeful face of Elk. "There is a young Kiowa called Sun Shadow, who is a better roper of antelope — " he said in his teasing Cheyenne way.

Elk laughed. " This Cheyenne is a catcher of horses, not antelope," also making light of it.

But Horsecatcher was not to be treated so. He told of two Comanche girls who roped antelope for fun, just to let them go again. They also caught wild mustangs right out of the herds, without even one throw of the rope. The story made Elk think less of a pair of young Cheyennes and a little more of the far Comanche camps, with some interest beyond their famous herds.

The next week was a busy one for Young Elk. At last both his father and Owl spoke no more of warring to him, and Two Wolves went out on a hunt without trying to coax his brother along. Instead, Elk was free to sit with Horsecatcher in the shade of the cottonwoods and listen to stories of the time when the old man first earned his name. Now and then Elk could see something of the far reaches of the man's mind and heart, as a sun breaks through a cloud momentarily — something of the horse-cunning in the old Indian, the man-wisdom.

With the growing moon Elk started out to find the golden stallion he had seen with Yellow Wolf, but now for the first time he went openly. Elk River walked beside his son to the edge of the village. It was evening, with the cooking fires like many fine red stars along the shadowed foot of the bluffs, the smoke rising slowly into the sun still golden over the tableland. The Elk saw Owl and Horsecatcher among the men in the evening council circle that his father had just left. His brother was coming in from a hunt, his sister out on a slope in a stick game. Red Sleeve was down at the water path where the young men waited for a gay word with her and the other maidens walking so demurely under the watchful eyes of the old women of the lodges. Elk saw all these, and made a parting picture of it to carry in his mind. Then he mounted his horse, and his father lifted a hand in good wishes, the left hand, the one nearest the heart.

On Horsecatcher's advice, Elk picked up an extra horse at his father's herd, one that carried well, and then started to the salt cliffs of the south. It was in country thick with Kiowas and Comanches, and when one could not go with a powerful war party the next best thing was to slip along in darkness and hide through the days in brushy gullies. It would take luck, a sharp eye and ear, and the good sense of his old dun mare and her pack sister, with perhaps the watchful help of the bird with horses. The salt-cliff country was very dangerous because so much big game came there to lick, even with the water very bad.

Elk approached the place after moonset, coming in cautiously along the bluff edge to avoid the great herd of resting buffaloes both above and below the salt slide, the dark hulks vaguely black in the starlight, their grunting and snuffing plain even when they couldn't be seen.

Although he had just washed himself and his clothing carefully and rubbed himself with badger oil against the man smell, some sharp-nosed cow detected him and started to run, and almost at once all the valley below him was a rumbling darkness, and then the tableland above him too, with only the shake of the earth to tell him the direction of the stampede or if the steep bluff where Elk clung would split the herd thundering around him. The roar of their grunting, the rancid, greasy smell of their wool were upon him, but passed in a dark flowing on both sides of the bluff point. Then they were gone and the only sound was of some wolves and coyotes, always skulking around the drags of a big herd, snarling over the cripples. Elk crept out carefully, listening, aware that enemies might have stampeded the buffaloes, not he. But there were only the wolves, and the sound of the nighthawk diving upon mosquitoes.

The young Indian felt cautiously down the overhang of the cliff for the rock face that it protected, slick, feeling wettish in the night air, and salt on his finger tips. With his little belt ax he cut out a large block, chopping very carefully, softly. Several times he froze to the cliff face, but the movement he heard was only some little night creature, and the owl's hoot, not from a wearer of Kiowa feathers.

At last he had several large lumps of rock salt in his hide sack. Back at his horses, he divided the load to both sides of the pack saddle and started westward. At dawn he settled for sleep in a canyon thick with plum and chokecherry brush, his horses tied close together on a grazing rope under some scrub trees, the end in his hand. He awoke at a whinnying of the dun mare and was up at once, his hand over the nose, and looked anxiously out over the valley. There, about a mile off, was a trailing of at least forty Indians riding in their dust. Elk held the nose of the pack horse too, and quieted himself. He was certain those Indians hadn't seen him yet, but there would surely be scouts out all around. He glanced up along the canyon rim, and there on the ridge high above him rode two Indians, and off across the valley two more.

The Cheyenne stood in his little clump of brush and trees, holding himself motionless, speaking softly to the horses, clinging to their noses. A long time the men stopped above him, and then they signaled mirror flashes, and started down the spine of the ridge toward the main party. All Elk could do was think of horses, fill his mind with nothing but horses as he had dreamed them — and the little bird riding their withers. The Indians were probably Kiowas, but he dared not look closely, afraid of the

57

eye's power to draw the eyes. Slowly they rode down and on past him, perhaps only to torture this foolish lone Cheyenne with hope and then to turn and strike. Or perhaps they had signaled to some that were coming behind to help surround him and the others that he must surely have with him. Perhaps they planned to grow hope and then trample it with their Kiowa humor, torment him to make a great laughing for them all.

The party had a fine string of horses, ridden and led, selected for the colors of drying prairie — yellows, duns, brown-roans, and claybanks. Elk watched them wind around a far ridge and out of sight, and then the scouts too. There seemed to be no more to follow, but Elk did not dare to release his struggling, impatient horses to graze again. Dusk finally came and he rode out to find water to quench his thirst from the chokecherries he had eaten. The older mare smelled it out, shaking her head against the rope that would draw her the other way. Later in the bit of moon that was pale as a skimming of fall ice, Elk struck northwest. By morning he should have his salt in safer country where his enemies, too, must take care. He wondered about the Kiowas. Perhaps they thought he was one of a large party, or that his horses, unloaded, were wild ones hiding from flies, or worn-out ones turned loose. Perhaps the wind had carried their neighing away and they were never seen at all. Surely he started with luck.

It took two more days to locate the herd with the golden stallion. He had crawled to the top of a ridge to look over into a watered valley, and just below him three mares were rolling in a sandy spot and rising one after the other to shake themselves in a shower of sand. There were more horses around a water hole and in the shade of a little brushy timber. Several more came to roll, and finally a yellow horse, the stallion, too, while the mares began to string off along their trail, their husky colts lazily along

58

behind. By now Elk was so hungry he had to shoot a rabbit and roast it over a handful of coals. He regretted having to kill anything that walked or swam or flew, but if he managed to snare the stallion he would need the strength of a wrestler as well as the cunning of Old Horsecatcher.

He ate the browned, juicy meat, washed himself and his clothing in a stale, muddy pool to lessen the man smell, and hung a lump of salt in a skin sack from a cottonwood near the water. He cut slits in the sack and splashed it with water to send the salt smell on the wind. Then he made a little nest for himself in the branches over the salt and spread a loop among the leaves below him, well weighted to fall easily around the sack. He spread another loop on the ground under the hanging salt, the rope covered, the end tied to the tree. Afterward Elk settled down to wait, knowing it might be days or even a whole moon before the stallion could be drawn to the salt, although that was a long time to hope for no enemies around, with the buffaloes fattening for fall. Besides, the cottonwood leaves would soon be turning golden as the white man's money in the palm and then fall, exposing the watcher who would catch a golden horse.

Each day the horses had come into the valley and then stopped at some muddy ponds, looking toward the big water hole but afraid of the man smell, it seemed. Then on the fourth day the wind blew in with them, and they marched straight for the water that Elk was watching. They drank but spread out to graze. The next time the lead mare sniffed the air and was drawn to the salt, half circling the hanging sack of it, curious and cautious too. But finally she came and licked a bit, rolling her eyes, snorting, shying at a leaf's drop, and yet drawn back, still cautious. The Elk's heart began to beat, for the stallion was approaching too, testing the air at ground level and then higher, his nostrils flaring, his fine sinewy neck arched in challenge. Once he looked back to the other horses, all watching, and then all around the valley, but already so close that Elk could see the fire in the luminous eye. The youth's hands went numb on the rope, and his heart drummed so loud that the horse must surely hear. Yet the stallion came forward, reaching out, drawing back into himself, his feet unwilling to retreat. Then, slowly, as to an accustomed thing, he raised his head high to lick. Elk released the weighted loop. It fell and missed, but as the horse whirled a forehoof caught in the ground loop, and as he plunged away he hit the end of the rope and went down on his head and over. Young Elk gasped, afraid the fine neck was broken. But the horse was up immediately. He tried to run again and went down once more. The next time he stood, and as Elk came quietly down the tree the stallion watched, long teeth bared, his mane blowing in a silvery cloud over his defiant face.

By the time the sliver of fading moon lingered long after the night was gone, Young Elk came home riding the stallion, golden and shining, driving his father's two mares before him. There was a good greeting for the young Cheyenne, not like a returning warrior, but good. Even those who had little honor for horses recalled that not long ago the Elk had killed a Kiowa raider just outside of the village, and had been given a young warrior name, Kiowa Killer, for it, although none ever thought of it for him, not even his father.

Many came to admire the golden stallion, the chief's horse — Elk's family too, all but Two Wolves, who was away, out against the Kiowas with a big party of Bowstring warriors. When the fine new horse had been admired and well hobbled for the night, Horsecatcher sent for the Elk.

"My son," he said, and the way he sounded the words

60

made the youth's heart leap like a deer from the buck-brush, "My son, I think perhaps you have truly a catching hand."

And so it was settled, with Horsecatcher's graying little wife bringing a bowl of soup to the weary young man. "Eat," she said, "and there are your sleeping robes. We welcome our new son."

5

THERE had been sad and terrible trouble in the village while Young Elk was away. Sometime before, a Cheyenne had killed a fellow tribesman and, as was necessary, the man was driven out, ostracized, for the required four years. His wife and relatives decided to go with him. He was a noted war chief, and so several young warriors went along. This small party must now live among all their enemies without tribal protection, and so would need the help.

But nothing is ever ended, as Elk River reminded his son. The red blanket of blood spilled upon the ground by a brother Cheyenne had defiled the Sacred Arrows, the gift of Sweet Medicine, their culture hero, who had brought many of the laws and the ceremonials to the people. Now the Arrows must be purified before any large undertaking of the people could hope to be successful, particularly a large war expedition.

But the Bowstring warriors were anxious to go to war against the Kiowas and wanted the Arrows renewed at once. They went to the Keeper, Gray Thunder. He protested that this could not be done quickly or whenever it pleased them. There were ceremonials to be made, and the time was not right. " Wait," he advised. " It will be better if you wait."

Angrily the impatient Bowstrings ordered Gray Thunder to purify the Arrows at once, and when he said it could not be done, they struck the seventy-year-old man down with their quirt handles. Everyone in the village ran out and stood in shocked and helpless silence, but no one dared interfere, for the Bowstrings were very powerful and they had cunningly chosen a time when the strong and independent men were away.

Finally the old man picked himself up from the dust and agreed to make the purifying ceremony, but he warned that they would have bad luck the first time they went out. There was also another warning from the village dreamer. He had seen bloody heads come into camp with their eyes shut, their skulls naked — scalped and bloody Cheyenne heads.

Many people were alarmed by these warnings, but the Cheyennes can be very obstinate and headstrong, Elk River told his son. One of the little war chiefs of the Bowstrings was very anxious for coups and honors. He harangued them to follow his moccasin tracks, and against him all the more moderate voices were as the winds of yesterday. " Why should we not go? " he shouted, tall and fierce in the light of the big fire built up in the center of the village. " A man can die only once. Would you live to be old men and ride helpless in the pony drags behind the old women? "

So they made up a small party of Bowstrings, including two who had been Elk's close friends several years ago, even last year. Then their paths had forked and he had become a chaser of horses, or horse tracks. The war party included four high-spirited youths eager for their first coup to do the camp work and, to amuse them, a man of the Contrary Society, those who do all things backward to make the people laugh, even if their hearts are on the ground. Before they had walked very far with their weapons and their ropes they were met by other small groups that had slipped away, until there were around forty men, all Bowstrings, all determined to strike south against the Kiowas or the Comanches for horses and some good fighting.

From the start it was like the darkness of a hailstorm hanging over them. The game was very wild for men afoot, and although they shot away many of their arrows they got little meat, and so were happy to run into Young Elk. He had been very grieved to hear what had happened in the village while he was gone for the golden horse, with his brother in the warrior society whose disrespectful and violent acts could only bring sorrow upon the people. He had taken two of his horses from the family herd and ridden out. " Not far, do not go far in this evil time, my son," the Horsecatcher's wife had said to him as she tied a small bladder of her very good pemmican to his belt.

Now, with the two horses and a mule that he had picked up on the prairie, Elk met the Bowstring party. They said nothing of their plans to him, but their cooking fires were bare until Two Wolves and another man rode Elk's horses out for buffalo and came back loaded with meat. In gratitude they offered to take Young Elk along, and were annoyed when he made the silent sign for " no." He wanted to go back home.

Two Wolves spoke out quietly, so quietly that only Elk knew the deep anger behind the words. " Our brother is too shy to say yes," Wolf told them. " His respect for the great fighters here has made him feel small, stolen his tongue. He will come."

But the youth did not change his mind, and in the silent way that his brother turned from him, Elk knew how much he had offended Two Wolves, and perhaps injured the young warrior's standing with the Bowstrings forever. He looked back from the crest of the first ridge, wishing he might have said something to ease the sorrow of this cold parting from his brother. But the Bowstrings were already moving too, slipping along the brushy creek bed, strung out, the youths of the party carrying the buffalo meat, dried, for they must save their few arrows, so few that Elk gave them all in his quiver and yet it was not enough for a really good fight.

A new moon fattened and died with no news at all of the Bowstring party. Then some young Sioux stopped by. They had been south to see a little of the world as was good before a man settles to village life. They brought a story that could not be believed and then had to be believed because there would never be another.

The Sioux had stopped outside of the Cheyenne village making warning signals that they carried news that was not good. They were brought in anyhow, welcomed and fed in the proper guest way. Then the men went to the fire at the Bowstring lodge and told their story, with people drawing near from all the village, coming on silent feet, afraid to listen, afraid not to hear.

The Kiowas had told them of a party of Bowstring warriors who spied out their main camps although very well hidden in a deep canyon. At dawn the Cheyennes sent two scouts to the edge of the bluffs to see what they could discover. But an early Kiowa starting out to hunt happened to notice what looked like the heads of two Indians against the paling sky. He rode up nearer to see. The Cheyennes, hoping to stop any alarm, sent their arrows against him. His horse went down, but recovered and got the Kiowa safely away.

At his first whoop of warning the warriors of his camp grabbed their arms and charged up to the bluffs. They found only a few moccasin tracks, impossible to follow on dry grass. They spread out to search the prairie and the breaks and finally gave up. But when they were returning to camp they saw a mirror signal from the Cheyennes. One bold and foolish young warrior let them see the flash of light to show his bravery, and then raised up to wave his blanket, daring the Kiowas to come and fight. They came, hundreds of them, riding, and surrounded the Bowstrings in some rocks, and when the Cheyenne powder was gone and the last of their arrows, the Kiowas charged and killed them all, losing only six of their own men. They took the scalps but did not strip the men of their clothing, for they had died bravely if very foolishly.

"Ah-h-h, foolish it truly was!" Ridge Tree cried in sorrow. "Thirty-eight Cheyennes dead because some Bowstrings went against the warnings of a man like Gray Thunder and his Sacred Arrows, so arrogant they braved the main Kiowa camps without sufficient arms!"

The Sioux seemed not to hear this. They said that the period of mourning for the six Kiowas killed was over when they came visiting there, just in time for the great victory dance, the greatest ever seen in that tribe, with the Bowstring scalps hanging from the women's staffs.

As the Sioux told these things their news spread over the push of men crowding up to hear. Among the women butcher knives flashed, hair was hacked off, arms and legs cut to bleeding, and a great keening began to rise like dark smoke from all the valley as night came on. Young Elk's mother and all his women relatives gashed themselves and hunched over the cold ashes of their cooking fires, crying thin and high for the beloved young Two Wolves. At almost every fire of the village it seemed the same, the men loosening their hair too, going ragged, singing the mourning songs.

But Elk could make no sound, no move to throw ashes into his hair or cut and slash his clothing to tatters. He could not even go near Bear Colt for comfort. Instead he ran into the breaks and sat bowed upon himself in a little

66

washout, alone all night and the next day except when the little captive white girl came by, with several small Cheyennes. She walked as solemnly as the others but could not be drawn on as easily when she saw the youth alone. Instead she stopped, held out her hands full of ripe sand cherries.

"Take," she said softly, and suddenly the water ran from Young Elk's eyes like a spring broken loose, water running over the dark stone of his face.

Runners were sent out to all the Cheyennes, even far up beyond the Platte, and soon the camps began to move together to make a great mourning for all those strong young warriors lost. But Young Elk was not there. He had slipped away southward, taking only his little bow, his knife, the rope about his waist, and a folded skin sack tied to his back. He sneaked past the Ute camps making their fall hunt, and when the country became very dry he went back to where he had seen some mustangs with a lone mare and her young colt hanging around the edges. She had old back sores, was evidently turned loose to heal by someone. She was of a gentle bay color and easy to catch, even lowered her head for the jaw rope, and seemed happy to be tame again. On her Elk headed down to the region where the Bowstrings had probably died, keeping out of sight as well as he could, watching for buzzards circling. He saw several, but all he found the first time was two buffaloes caught in an old mudhole, bloated like little round mountains. The next time he found the dead Cheyennes, their bones scattered along the little ravines where they had been killed. He made himself look upon them as upon strangers, walking here and there, dragging the long skin sack as for the gathering of buffalo chips. Finally he found the bones of his brother, knowing them by the moccasins of his mother's making still tied to the ankles. He gathered the bones into the sack and carried them to a creek bluff. There he laid them into a hollow under the rocks and covered the place well with loose boulders. Then he sat beside it a long time, wondering if he had somehow taken the wrong road when he decided to become a horsecatcher. Perhaps his brother might still be alive if the family honor had not pressed so heavily upon his young shoulders alone. It was hard for the son of two great warrior lines to have nothing but a brother who caught horses. So Two Wolves had needed to be very brave and doubly bold.

But there was one thing Young Elk could do — bring back a good horse, one he would call by his brother's name so he might speak it freely, without disrespect for the one he had loved as part of himself.

After a day and night of fasting beside the grave in the rocks, the Elk wandered down to the little stream for a drink. Then he remembered the need for caution because a bird made a sudden shrill *teering* sound and flew up and away. Without moving, as still as he would be with an approaching mustang herd and as sharp-eared, he turned only his eyes and looked along the bluffs, up the creek and then down.

Behind a little bush at the bluff top an Indian was watching. He was well hidden, but the horse hunter's sharpened eyes saw him and knew that, alone and with only a handful of rabbit arrows, he would have to be very sly and quick to get away. True, the little bird had made its warning cry for him, showing that the Powers would be with him if he were wise enough. He realized now that Old Horsecatcher and surely his father and Owl would all have known that the Kiowas were watching these bones for those who came to give them respectful burial. Yet here a foolish young horse lover came, sneaking away without one sip at the deep springs of wisdom right at home.

For a full heart's beat, or so it seemed, Elk managed to make himself an empty thing, hollow and without rim, feeling invisible. But only one moment, and then he was once more a Cheyenne stupidly trapped by a watching Kiowa, perhaps even ten, twenty of them. With a last glance all around the rim of the creek bluffs for more enemies, for a way to escape, Elk eased himself back from the water and, like a flowing snake, crept over into the fanning mouth of a gully. Stooped low, he slipped along under the bank, thankful he had seen the Kiowa while still not too close. There were surely others, but for now he must avoid the danger he could see. He moved very fast until he struck a little stretch of brush about twice knee-high and was crawling into this very cautiously, careful to touch no stalk or stem that could carry a quiver to the top, when he heard words almost at his head. There was a reply from the other side, and a running, and now Elk dared not move to look but lay as much a part of the brush shadow as he could. The men were afoot, scouting the sides of the gully, moving toward the creek, evidently unable to believe that the Cheyenne had reached so near the top of the bluff so soon. They scouted carefully, moving back and forth, coming into the range of Elk's eyes as he watched from under his sheltering arm, the little sliver of black glass from his dreaming pressing into his ear as he clung close to the earth. The men were almost past him now, each one watching for any sign on the opposite side of the gully, looking for tracks too, and once more Elk was thankful for grass, the sodded grass of the earth that could accept his crawling weight and betray no memory of his passing.

Several times the men stopped to look back up the slope and beyond, perhaps for companions to come. Now Young Elk had to risk everything and make the short run over the crest and try to get to his horse if the mare had not already been found.

Little bird, little bird — he thought, and then while the men thrashed around in the rushes of the creek he ran, stooping almost double.

But one Kiowa saw Elk as he went over the top and fell flat. With a whooping the Indian started up the slope. Elk took one swift look around. East, down the creek, two horses waited, heads together, loads of fresh meat on their backs. Nothing else was in sight, and if these two were alone, and if his mare was still undetected, perhaps —

Young Elk rose and, still shielded by the bluff from the men climbing it, ran west for the head of another gully. He went along the ragged cut, keeping low, running bent to the earth. Once the Kiowas saw him and while one sprinted for him the other went for their horses. Zigzagging, in and out of the breaks, dodging among the weeds and brush, Elk expected a bullet every moment, but finally he slid, played out, down the gravel slope of the box canyon to his picketed mare. She was standing, ears pointed to him, the colt sleeping as though no enemy lived anywhere.

Elk slashed the picket rope with his knife, jumped on the mare, and whipped to the creek and up the narrowing canyon, not leaving it so long as it led straight on, so the two men couldn't cut in on him. When the creek bent southward he turned up a gully and headed out northwest upon the tableland, all strange country. The only thing Elk knew of it was that he wouldn't be riding blindly into a Kiowa camp up on this dry plain.

The two men were whipping hard after him now, although still too far for all but the luckiest bullet, and while Elk's mare was not young, she hadn't been chasing game today or carrying a heavy meat pack in addition to a big Kiowa. But the enemy gained, and the Cheyenne had to keep heading straight on no matter what lay before him, looking back to the Indians and to the colt, still running but certain to be lost soon. They would all be lost soon, Elk realized. He was whipping too now, the mare laboring, the Cheyenne hoping there were no open holes for her worn, clumsy feet, the Kiowas whooping just behind.

Then suddenly the pursuers stopped, and Elk skimmed the bare fall-hazed plain for the reason — perhaps other Kiowas ahead, or even some of their enemies. But there was nothing, not even an antelope or a coyote, no movement except the slowing gallop of his own mare. Then, almost at her stumbling feet, a dark brushy canyon opened, a deep gash cutting across the flat tableland, the steep canyon walls lost in the tangle of thicket and timber far below. Elk began to laugh. What a fine world for a man to live in! He wanted to sing about it, sing of the earth that opens like shielding arms to the fleeing. The Kiowas had known that even this very foolish Cheyenne could save himself here.

When Elk returned, the village was gone once more, with sticks laid to show the move to the South Platte. He followed very slowly, resting the mare, working with the colt that was fattening again, even after the wearing run from the Kiowas. Elk watched the sky for the pale morning smudge of many cooking fires, and so he found the camp, a great one now, and in deep mourning, the women with freshly gashed legs, his mother grieving for two sons lost. She welcomed Elk quietly, but as one returned from the burial rocks, for everyone had known he had gone to rescue the bones of his brother. Without the wily training of a warrior, the Elk would surely be caught as easily as a rabbit is grabbed by the wolf. His sister had been mourning him too, and his new mother, the wife of Horse-catcher. She alone was free to speak her affection. "Ah-h-h, son, it is good to see you are living!" she cried.

It was also good that Elk had returned in time for the formal tribal mourning. Every day more of the Cheyenne

71

bands were coming in for the ceremonials and to plan the avenging. Always the women and the old men walked ahead of the rest, wailing and weeping, those behind them riding without the finery or any of the gaiety of a moving camp. Formally they set their lodges in the great tribal circle, each in the proper place of the ten bands that made up the Cheyenne nation.

After the newcomers had their lodges up, their warriors came over the top of a hill as in a war charge, but in ceremonial paint and in all their formal regalia, and all the fine war bonnets, the quilled, beaded, and scalped-locked shirts, the fine-tailed breechclouts, the leggings with beads and bells and silver down the sides. So, with their shields up, their feathered lances and the few guns lifted high, they charged down upon the camp, whooping and shooting. Just before they reached the great circle they turned off to the side and rode past. Once more they lined up, by warrior societies this time, two and four abreast, and came back to circle the village, going one way and then the other. Finally they rode in at the opening, and settled into the camp. The next day another village came, and then another, until it seemed that every Cheyenne in the world was there.

Always the talk turned to the men who would help avenge the dead. To all the newcomers this included Young Elk, who had gone so boldly all alone to rescue the bones of his brother. This one whose name was really Kiowa Killer should be given a good place in the expedition of revenge. To this talk the father was silent, making himself ready for the fighting, as though he were the only man of the family, almost as though he had no son left at all.

When the Cheyennes had all arrived, a large brush arbor was built in the middle of the great circle for the warrior societies. Here all who had lost relatives in the

72

Bowstring party brought horses and other presents. They came close to the long row of warriors and passed their hands over the faces of the men, asking them to take pity, to avenge their loved ones. The blood running down the arms of the mourning women left the red of it on the warrior faces until they seemed fierce and wild as from a great fight already made. Afterward an old man rode slowly around the camp, calling out the names of the soldier bands the sacred four times, because that was the number of the Great Directions. Then he called on all the brave young men who had not joined the warrior societies too, and after each call he repeated the same thing: "The presents that have been gathered are all for you who avenge our beloved men."

At first there had been kindly looks toward Young Elk from those of the other bands, because they knew he had a brother killed. But the looks from most of Elk's acquaintances were like the snow winds and made the heat of shame come up in his face. When his mother, too, walked before the warriors to touch them with bloody hands and beg them to avenge her son, Elk could not bear to see it. He stumbled away, out past Red Sleeve, and had to know that she drew her blanket up on that side to hide her face so she need not see this cowardly one.

When these ceremonials were finished the Crier told the people that the chiefs had decided what must be done. "The warriors will prepare their war bonnets and their medicine ornaments, their shields and their weapons!" he called out all around the great camp so everyone could know. But while these preparations were made an early snow swept in from the north, deep snow that lay like sleep over all the plains until it was very hard to get enough meat for so many together, with too little grass for the great cloud of horses even before the snow came. Soon all the cottonwood bark for the horses was gone, and even Young Elk couldn't keep the herds of his two fathers strong, although he lived with them most of the time, seeking out wind-swept slopes, squatting for hours beside the shaggy, winter-haired Bear Colt and the golden stallion as they pawed the drifts. It helped keep a few horses strong enough to carry hunters for deer and antelope for Elk's two families and for some who had no hunters left.

There was suffering from cold too, with wood scarce and the buffalo chips deep under snow. All winter they saw not one buffalo, and many were certain this was caused by the double defilement of the Sacred Arrows. Wasn't it true that the herds left if the women lost their virtue? Then why not if the Arrows lost their power?

By the time it seemed that the tribe would really face starvation, with many eating their horses, the buffaloes were suddenly there again, and as soon as the pony drags could move through the shrinking drifts, the camp split up. With meat made, and the robes tanned by the women, they went to Bent's Fort for supplies — coffee and sugar that they had not tasted for many moons, and Hudson Bay guns, and flints, powder and ball — for although all the Cheyenne tribe was here, the Kiowas were more powerful.

Finally everything was done and all but a small party of relatives of the Cheyenne woman married to Bent were gathered at the Arkansas River. Here the songs of the dedicated ones were sung. One after another of the men walked about the great circle behind the announcing Crier, pledging himself to the avenging. With his lance and arrows or his gun, and in full regalia and paint, he sang the death song, the song of No Returning. One had a wife and two small children, but he took no pity on them, singing that he must go. Another was the son of

74

the dead leader of the Bowstrings, a youth no older than Elk. As this one passed around the circle, Red Sleeve and many others looked to where the one named Kiowa Killer stood, and even some of Elk's relatives looked too, and all he could do was slip away into the crowd once more.

"It is a test of your call," Horsecatcher said to the miserable youth come to stand before him, shamed and torn between the two roads that still demanded his feet. "Through these things you will know." The old man spoke without lifting his eyes from his pipe, giving no advice, no sign this way or that.

Plainly there was no place for the hesitation of Young Elk in this gathering for tribal vengeance. With his horse rope about his waist and the meat and extra moccasins that Horsecatcher's wife ran to bring, he slipped away toward the hills. No one except this new mother seemed to see him go. She stood looking after the tall young man, as handsome in his plain clothing as the gaudiest village dandy. But there was one bit of adornment besides the sliver of black glass and the feather tied behind his ear. His long shining braids were wrapped in plain bands of colt skin against the tearing of brush and briers, but she had made a bit of beading for the ends — little bead pictures of the bird of Elk's dreaming as he had told it sitting beside her as she worked. Because she was his second mother, she could let this youth sit with her and tease her as his blood mother never could without trapping the son of her breast for all his lifetime.

So now Horsecatcher's wife stood a long time looking after Young Elk, throwing her heart to the Powers for help for him, so he would grow into the man the people must have. She was still standing there when Elk had his horse. From far off he raised his hand to her and then rode away southward alone.

6

*W*HEN the avenging ceremonies were all done, the chiefs decided that no Kiowa prisoners were to be taken. Not one of the Bowstrings had been spared. With this dark purpose on the heart, the camp started southward, silent, even the children reflecting the grave faces of their elders like ponds under darkened skies. Many scouts were sent out, two at a time. The first ones ran into Young Elk watching along their probable path. Now he was not seen; he saw them. This much he had learned.

His horse-hunting had gone miserably, he said. This country was too open, too well-watered, and the horses were very wild, as though they had been chased lately, probably by Kiowas, he had thought. So he picked up a trail that turned out to be of a party of horsecatchers going home. He followed them clear to their village, moving, but too large to be going very far, and making long stops. There were Comanches near too, probably going to the same place.

"Ah-h-h!" the two scouts said, pleased. "You have the eye of the lone traveler." They had seen a small Kiowa hunting party too, and were almost caught by it. Now they would go back to the people with Elk to report.

But Young Elk stayed out. "I will watch," he said.

The others murmured their "*Hou!*" of approval, knowing why he did not return. "We will tell Red Sleeve you are in great danger," one said, and laughed softly as they slipped away into the night. Elk knew how it would be, the formal spreading of the news that he had discovered. All the skin lodges would be left standing as though everybody were not far away, except that there would be platforms built for everything that the wolves might destroy. Then they would start in the night, so no skulking Kiowa could see them go. Gray Thunder and his wife, Young Elk's aunt, would be carrying the Sacred Arrows along, but sorrowfully, because they were still unpurified from their defilement, and not yet avenged.

All night the Cheyennes marched southward. No one, perhaps not even the waiting Young Elk, could guess just where the main Kiowa camp would be. Elk realized he must not risk detection and perhaps give the enemy a hint of the coming attack, let them prepare an ambush that could destroy the Cheyenne nation. He watched the direction of parties returning with meat and horses, even some Comanches going the same general path, perhaps camped near their Kiowa allies. With these things in his mind, Elk slipped back and got into the moving Cheyenne columns at night. He was immediately surrounded by the more reckless warriors anxious to be the first to strike an enemy, to count the first coup — those who had to be watched night and day to keep them from slipping out ahead. One of these foolish ones might also betray the attack and bring not only failure but ambush and death to many, many of the helpless ones along. So far none had eluded the warriors of the society that was policing the march. Horseback, these men kept the marching strings surrounded all night, watching, and protecting the older people and the women who were afoot because this way their treading was lighter upon the earth for any listening ear. They went slowly, leading the horses with packs and with the drags for the sleeping children, the old, and the sick. At dawning they split into smaller parties and hid over the day.

Then before daylight one morning, a party of seven Cheyennes discovered some Kiowa men and women going out to hunt buffaloes. The scout who saw them signaled the Cheyennes down. Then on a ridge in plain sight of the Kiowas he threw his lance to stand in the earth and rode back and forth in the sign for " Buffaloes have been seen."

Apparently the Kiowas thought he was one of their scouts and rode toward him on their traveling horses, still leading their fast hunters, yet hurrying because the Cheyenne decoy kept looking off over the prairie as though watching a moving herd. When the Kiowas were so close he could hear their voices, he grabbed up his lance and charged them, the rest of the Cheyennes upon them too. Surprised, the Kiowas had no time to change to their fast horses to escape or even to get their bows out of the saddle cases. The Cheyennes lanced them and shot them down until all of the thirty were dead and the horses captured. One brave Kiowa might have escaped. He got upon his fast horse and was almost away, but his wife was crying for help, and he charged back to her and was also killed.

This should have been a good beginning in the avenging, a very brave beginning. One man killed twelve Kiowas, another got eight. But the little party were the ostracized Cheyennes, the ones driven out of camp because the leader had killed a fellow tribesman in a fight over trader whisky and brought defilement upon the Sacred Arrows. It was after this that the Bowstrings had whipped the Arrow Keeper and compelled him to make a hurried purification ceremony and then were lost. So the thirty dead Kiowas did not count in the avenging, but

78

it was good to know that the little party of the ostracized were still living, strong and well.

A little later the great Cheyenne war camp found the main village of the Kiowas and charged from the lower end of it because frightened people and horses always flee downward, downhill, downstream. Young Elk had stayed back on a far ridge with the older women and the young children, his bow drawn, ready like those of the boys and the old men guarding their helpless ones. Elk was uneasy at this killing to come but tried to act ready for defense. No one looked at him, perhaps because there was the fighting to watch far off. In spite of himself Elk drew nearer, telling himself that if the Cheyennes and some Arapaho friends who came up to help were whipped, the Kiowas would attack from his direction. Much nearer were many younger women and girls like Red Sleeve and his sister, watching along rises, to cheer, to sing strong heart songs for the warriors.

It was hard to see much of the fighting because the dust and the smoke from grass and lodges burning was very thick. Elk did see that some of the Kiowa women had saddled their fastest horses and were loading them to flee, while others hacked out battle pits with their butcher knives and threw up breastworks. It was here that the young Cheyenne warriors, those who had sung the Never-Return songs, showed their bravery. They jumped over these barriers and avenged their relatives over and over before they died. But the fighting lasted a long time, and even those back on the far ridge knew that many good men of the Cheyennes must be dying down there — not only the dedicated ones and some daring young warriors who jumped the breastworks with them, but many others too, killing and dying in the fight that scattered along the bottoms and over the up-

79

lands of Wolf Creek. Comanches hurried in to help, and some of them were killed too and much blood lay on the ground.

Then suddenly a great Cheyenne crying went up, and was echoed back, back, until it reached the farthest ridge, with a high and thin keening above all the fight. The Keeper of the Sacred Arrows had been run over in the wild charge. The wise and honored Gray Thunder was dead, dead. First the Bowstrings were all destroyed down here after they had struck the Keeper. Now there was this greater sign of the violation put upon the Arrows to sweep like a blizzard wind over every Cheyenne heart.

When the Keeper of the Sacred Arrows fell, his wife was nearby, as was her duty. As was also her duty, she did not stop to mourn or even to compose the face of her man. Instead, she grabbed up the Arrows, and with them secured as a child in the blanket on her back she slipped through the dust and roar of the fighting, scuttling from weed to brush to washout, with several Kiowas hard after her.

Young Elk saw his aunt go and whipped out to help her, but he rode from a gully straight upon two Kiowas searching the breaks for her. They started shooting and Elk's horse went down. He landed running, and although a bullet grazed his head he made it back into the gully and slipped up it like a weasel through a brush patch. Afoot now, he could not hope to help the Keeper's fleeing wife, perhaps not even find her, if she was not already dead. But he had to watch the prairie, his eyes moving back and forth. Far out he saw an Indian slip like a shadow over an exposed rise into a farther break. Elk started to run, letting the warnings of those behind him fall to earth.

By evening Elk had followed the woman over sandy hillets, bare gravel breaks, and up long snake-head gullies, even through a scattering of browsing buffaloes that some-how scarcely moved out of her way. He finally overtook her, but it was not easy. Under a vow to protect the Arrows with her life, and to flee with them so long as the moccasin could lift itself from the earth, she had traveled very fast, and when Young Elk finally caught up she flattened herself upon the prairie as skillfully as a young quail loses itself in the grass. Although he had seen her vanish, he could not discover her hiding; not until he gave up and called softly, "Aunt, oh, Aunt, it is your foolish nephew of the horses —" did she move. She sat up peering from dust-caked eyes at him as she rubbed her bleeding feet one moment before running on.

"You must rest; eat a little and rest," the young man urged. "I will help; I will watch."

But nothing would hold her. The enemy could catch her as easily as he had done, easier, with horse and gun. So Young Elk gave her the spare moccasins tied to his back and then jogged along beside her, keeping up, as the young can for a while, yet wondering how this wife of the old Arrow Keeper could move so fast and so long, with such breath-bursting runs over exposed ground. When her legs would no longer bear her, she sank down, but in a few moments she was off again like a startled deer. Each time Elk caught himself looking back more carefully, certain she had seen pursuit, must know it was near. And as he ran he saw that not all the courage, all the brave heart, was back there among the fighters. Perhaps this was a stronger thing here, and done without fighting, without blood upon the ground, as was fitting, since the great power of the Arrows was for good, good grass and fat buffaloes, healthy villages, victory, and happy, peaceful times for the people.

But these thoughts were interrupted by a flock of ravens suddenly flying up from somewhere ahead, going up like dark leaves in a whirlwind. Elk caught his aunt and pulled her down into the thin scattering of stunted sagebrush as a small string of Indians, all men leading war horses, climbed up on the tableland. There was not even a washout or a buffalo wallow, nothing to do but flatten motionless to the ground.

"Earth, we are part of you," the Arrow Keeper's wife said softly over and over, "Earth, we —"

The Indians came straight on toward them, perhaps headed to a camp already set up by scouts, for a whiff of new fire rode the south wind. Slowly the Indians neared — enemy Comanches who would be very happy to capture the famed Cheyenne Arrows tied to the back of an old woman in a bare withering of gray sagebrush.

It was a long, long time before they were past, and when there seemed no others following, Young Elk helped the woman to her feet. Once more they started northward over the evening prairie, the woman stumbling in weakness. "We must eat," Elk said, and the Keeper's wife unfolded her blanket and held up a large rattlesnake with the head chopped off. "He was across my path when I was crawling —" she said, half apologetically. So they built a little fire, no bigger than a palmful of sagebrush twigs, and roasted the skinned snake. It was a good time for this, the golden sun blinding in its slant across the tableland, and with the smell of another fire on the wind. Afterward Elk said he was turning back. "If you will keep toward our old crossing, I will try to get horses."

"Ah-h-h, my son, be very careful! These Comanches are good warriors —"

Elk realized that, and also that he was no warrior at all with only a little bow and a knife. But he was a horse-catcher, and sometimes that meant taking horses from the enemy. Silently he melted into the shadows and headed southward.

✿

Young Elk had more trouble finding the little Comanche camp than he had expected. By now everyone knew of the many Cheyennes loose in the south country, their trail wide and plain to see. But hidden camps can be found, and so Elk drove the point of his thin steel knife into the ground and put his ear to its high little song. He could catch no movement close by, but off east a way there seemed some starting and stopping, like large animals feeding, but the feet faster than a scattering of buffaloes in the night. He slipped eastward, moistening the inside of his nose for smoke, sharpening his ears, and keeping down below the crests of the ridges. After a while he saw a spot of flame, barely half a finger high. Silently he crept around it but he could see no shadows, no movement, and then suddenly he realized what it was, a decoy fire, to get him to come sneaking up to see, just as he did, and so show himself up dark against the fire for the watchers far out. He flattened to the mesquite grass but it was too late. Something was upon him from behind, and Young Elk went down hard under a cracking blow.

A long, long time afterward the Elk heard a groaning that cut through his head like the blade of a Cheyenne war ax. There was something bright and hot as fire at his nose, and when he tried to move back, he couldn't get his hands or feet loose. Slowly his head cleared and he looked around the coals close before his face. Several men were there smoking, Comanches by the look of their clothing and hair, Comanches with their dark eyes upon their captive.

"Our young Cheyenne friend was very easy to catch," the headman said, in sign talk. "Our young men learn earlier —"

Anger swelled in Elk's throbbing head. Even here there was ridicule. "I am a catcher of wild horses," he finally told them, making the signs in the narrow space that his bound hands permitted, but not telling how few he had caught.

The men laughed. "Do you always find them around fires in the night? And who is with you — where is your party?"

"I am alone. I slip out alone," the Elk said quickly, as was true, but wondering about the Arrow Keeper's wife. Had they been watching her too?

They said no more to him, and after a little work with some scalps they had along, stretching the skins on willow hoops to dry at the night coals, one after another the men rolled into their blankets. Only Elk had none. He was already shivering and hungry as a wolf now that his head hurt less. He wondered what would be done with him, since he wasn't killed at once. Would he be used to find what they must think was a party close by, or as a decoy? How stupid he was, and what more avenging this would cause his people when it was finally discovered. But that might be many moons, or never, if his aunt who ran with the Arrows did not get away.

The night grew chillier, and as Elk tried to slide himself silently around to get more of his body to the warmth of the dark fire spot, he saw a bit of redness still glowing at the outer edge of the ashes. Holding his breath to its regular pattern in his excitement, he glanced around the starry darkness to the sleeping men and beyond them to where the hobbled horses were feeding, surely under guard. No one stirred, the only sound a burrow owl and some far wolves, snarling, perhaps over a fat buffalo carcass.

Elk knew he must work fast now, with the redness in the ashes so very small. He turned upon his side, moving very cautiously, and reached out to draw the coal toward him with his bound hands, using the thong that held them together to drag it along, hoping to pull it under the cover of his breast before anyone awoke. "Earth, shield me —" he said to himself, knowing that if he was discovered, a war club would splatter his brain upon the ashes.

Once one of the men stirred, and Elk held himself still, even though the coal burned into his wrist instead of the rawhide thong, holding his hand still against the searing pain, hoping that there would be no stink of burning flesh. Gradually he managed to move himself a little farther over his hands, with the coal under the thong. He even blew down upon the ember a little, made it glow red as a rising moon seen through summer leaves. Now there was the stink of scorching rawhide. Slowly Elk counted his breath, so many numbers between each, making it regular and shallow as that of a sleeper, hoping he would not sneeze from the twist of smoke that tickled his nose as it crept out.

Slowly he pulled with his hands, hard, until his wrists were wet with blood, and bright sparks of light shot around under his lids. Then suddenly the thong broke and his hands flew apart, making a plain noise. He shifted quickly so the noise would seem to be that, yawned and stretched his bound legs, knowing that the Comanche ears would catch these movements. One of the men rose and came over to the Cheyenne. "Hungry, hungry," Young Elk complained, trying to sound half asleep. The man laughed a little, low but derisively, and said something to the others that Elk did not understand.

It was a long time before the camp seemed asleep again and the Elk dared blow on the dark coal shielded by his shirt, his only hope for breaking the thongs of his ankles. It was of a gnarled bit of root, still hot, and he blew softly, then harder, but the fire in its heart seemed dead. Finally he broke it, and in its blackness all his hope was gone. He would be killed for freeing his hands, or even if he lived as a captive and that was discovered, the Bowstrings would be bound to move, and there would be another tribal war, this one with the Comanches, and how could the Cheyennes survive such fighting with so many warriors as both the Comanches and the Kiowas?

Truly his father and Owl had spoken wisely in their fear for their young man when they tried to advise him. And perhaps somewhere off north an old Cheyenne woman was running this moment with the Sacred Arrows, running alone, weary to dropping, but going on and on, without food or sleep, and none to help her except Elk, the Elk who was given the unused name of Kiowa Killer, unused and unfitting for one who let the Comanches strip everything from him — bow, knife, rope, and fire flint.

Then suddenly Elk remembered something — the bit of stone tied behind his ear, the sliver of the black glass from the country of the steaming waters up the Yellowstone. It was only the size of a fingernail, but sharp as the white man's glass is sharp, and he had found it beside the feather of his dreaming.

Slowly he eased a hand up under his head and tore the cord with the stone loose. Then he drew himself together so his hands, as though still bound, could saw at the rawhide that tied his ankles. It would take a long time, and already a paleness was spreading along the east.

Twice he thought he had awakened the men, and once a scout came in to talk low to the leader. It must have been disturbing news, for someone ran out, apparently for the horses. Elk heard the Comanche word for " Cheyennes " and guessed the scout had seen the great camp that would pass not far from here on their way home. Between now and the dawning Elk must hurry, take chances. He sawed harder with the bit of stone, and by the time the horses were coming in the thong yielded, and as the dark forms of the horses came past, Elk sprang to his numbed feet and grabbed for a mane. He missed, but got a handful of hair on the next one. The horse shied from him, plunging sideways, and then stampeded from the Comanche shouting and alarm. But already Elk was on, clinging to the far side by a hand wrapped in the mane and a toe over the back, off in the shadowy dawning. Shots whistled past and then the pounding run of several horsemen followed him. But the Cheyenne had a good start on a fast horse, very sure-footed. By sunup he seemed safe, with a scattered bunch of buffaloes that he scared up running between him and the Comanches.

At a little creek Elk stopped to water his horse, a good sorrel, although a little thin from a long war expedition. While the horse grazed Elk clung to the mane and tore his white-man shirt into strips for a braided jaw rope. Then he headed northward, and by evening he found his aunt, still carrying the Arrows, moving, but with an aimless shamble as though wounded to dying. Her face was gaunt and sunken, the moccasins Elk had given her worn out, her feet bleeding and swollen thick from the cactus thorns. Although she was still moving when Young Elk caught her, she had to be lifted to the sorrel's back and tied on. Then Elk slapped the horse, and, running beside her, they started toward the Arkansas River and the Cheyenne country beyond.

7

*T*HE KEEPER'S wife slipped from the horse like a dead one when Young Elk untied her at the little camp of Cheyennes near Bent's Fort. The Elk was played out too. Even the horse doubled up his worn legs and stretched out in the dust right among the lodges.

People came running from all around to see what was happening, and then parted to let the two headmen through. They stopped when they saw it was Gray Thunder's wife, their faces suddenly bleak as winter.

"The Arrows they are safe," Young Elk said very quickly, to reassure the men, the people. But there was more that must be told. "Our good man is dead," he admitted in the shame of such news.

Dead? Dead! Dead. The word was said by one after another, like stones falling into water, and lost in the keening that swept over the little crowd. But the Keeper's wife did not hear this. She had to be carried to a lodge in a blanket, and when the women tried to feed her good meat soup it all seemed to run out of her mouth. The medicine healer came to make the chants and burn healing herbs in the lodge, to bathe the woman's feet, draw out the cactus, and rub on badger grease for the healing. And all through this the woman seemed in a dark dreaming.

By morning other Cheyennes had come in, small parties

that were unable to keep up on the hard march south and hurried back out of the enemy country. They were anxious about the fight too, and were waiting when Keeper's wife awoke. So, before she could make her mourning duties or even begin the keening for her sorrow, she had to be taken to the headmen to tell the story of the Arrows. In her soft Cheyenne she told of the fighting, with Gray Thunder keeping the Arrows back a little because they were still not cleansed, were still unrenewed. Then suddenly he was hit by a bullet, and she ran to save the sacred bundle and fled with it, enemy warriors following her hiding path. She told of Young Elk's horse getting shot and his run with her afoot. His good eye had caught the signal of the ravens when enemies were near, and after the Comanche party was past, he went into their night camp for horses and was captured. But he got away with a horse, evaded pursuit, and found her when it seemed she must take the Arrows to some hill and perhaps die there with them, for she could no longer lift the moccasin.

Now the Arrows must go to some good man until a new Keeper could be selected. Standing with the help of a medicine lance driven into the ground and with Young Elk to support her arm, she went through the ceremonial of temporary transfer.

Only then could she gash her arms and legs, tear her ragged dress in further tatters, and throw the ashes of despair into her loosened braids.

As soon as he could, Young Elk sneaked off to where the horses of his village were held by herders. The yearling Bear Colt stood away from the youth with the strange and disturbing smells of long hunger and fatigue upon him. But when Elk sat in the grass and began his low coaxing sounds, the Colt's ears sharpened, curious, and soon he came nosing up to nip at the black braids, nuzzle up underneath, until Elk had to push him away from the little feather bundle with the sliver of obsidian that had freed him from the Comanche captors.

Now finally Young Elk had time to wonder about his family and the Horsecatcher and the rest, still down south in Kiowa country, and about Red Sleeve. He wished the girl might have heard the generous words of the Arrow Keeper's wife, but with all the coups and scalps and other war honors, the admiration in the winsome face of Red Sleeve would be for the warriors, her gay dark eyes following them in the victory dancing.

Against these exploits what could a horsecatcher hope to offer, unless it was the white horse of the south, the stallion that was white as mist in morning sunlight. But that one no man could catch alive.

Perhaps because he was uneasy about the Cheyennes not yet home, or perhaps because the wild horses called to him, Elk got restless loafing around Bent's Fort with the other youths who raced their horses, wrestled, danced, and talked of the coups they would soon be counting. They said this looking toward the Elk, older than they, certainly old enough for coups long before this. So as soon as his ribs fatted a little, Young Elk wrapped his rope about his waist and slipped away, but returned to tie the Comanche horse beside the lodge where the Keeper's wife slept. The sorrel was rested now and plainly a special war horse, fast and very well trained, so well that when Elk's aunt went to sleep on the way north the sorrel had turned himself against her sliding weight, to keep her from overbalancing, falling. Then he shook himself a little and finally harder, pawing too, as though to jolt the rider awake.

"Ah-h-h, I must teach my horses to do this warrior thing," Elk had told himself, and almost wished that he could have been a captive of the Comanches awhile longer, long enough to taste of their ways with the wild mustangs and perhaps to see the two horse-catching sisters who were so highly honored among a horse-catching people.

After two days of easy travel Elk saw the thin dust of a great move hanging over the country ahead. It turned out to be the main body of the Cheyennes returning from the Kiowa fight. He signaled, and several Dog Soldiers, the warrior society in charge of the moving camp, came for him through the evening sun. He had no news for them except of the courage of the Keeper's wife and the safety of the Arrows. But all this they would know —

" *Hou!* " the headmen murmured over their pipes. They had had mirror signals from near Bent's that the Arrows were saved, but it was good to have it straight from the tongue.

Finally the Elk was free to go to the fire of his parents where there was sorrow for the dead Gray Thunder, and satisfaction too, in the strong avenging of Two Wolves, of all the Bowstrings.

"You will come back with us to receive honor for helping to save the Arrows, as the signals we received tell us," the father said.

But the son did not answer, and White Moccasin, in her sisterly innocence, had to tease a little. " It is known that the lodge of the red-sleeved one is with those gone ahead," she told her mother. " Our brother will be there."

The mother made the gesture of silence, and the girl looked down in her confusion, while Elk was told of the end of the fighting. Afterward he went away to the fire of Old Horsecatcher. Here he stretched out to rest, full of fresh roast buffalo from the big surround the camp had made yesterday. Here there was no talk of the fine avenging for the Bowstrings killed, and no one was in the tatters and ragged hair, although some beloved relatives had been killed in the fight. Instead, Elk listened all evening to stories of the mustang and of the few-water country where the wild ones were easiest to trap. There were stories of some particularly fine horses, both caught and still free, but there was no word of the White One.

"We would not have you go into the south country alone now," Old Horsecatcher said. "Too many have bad hearts that can only be made good again by red Cheyenne blood. Their eyes will be very sharp."

So Elk told a little about his capture by the Comanches. "Captured!" Horsecatcher exclaimed, and the hand of his wife flew to her mouth in alarm.

"I got away," Young Elk told them cheerfully, saying the obvious a little boastfully and bringing a secret smile of amusement to the face of his second mother.

"The Kiowas will not be taking captives now, nor perhaps the Comanches," Horsecatcher warned.

But Elk had gone in the darkness, slipping around to the west to avoid any vengeful enemy warriors trailing the Cheyennes for stragglers as wolves follow the buffalo herds. He was sorry to go without seeing Red Sleeve, but he could not have approached her lodge in this mourning time anyway. Perhaps when he returned and the victory dancing was all over —

"You will need very strong medicine to make a returning," the Horsecatcher had told him, speaking not as a second father but as one man to another.

"My friends the birds have many eyes," Elk had replied.

He was a little better prepared to go far from home this time, with an awl and sinews from the Catcher's wife, Many Moccasins, as she had named herself because, with a horse-catching husband, she had to make trailing moccasins in bunches like the grapes that hang so sweet from the vines after the frost. She showed Elk how to make durable foot covering from the pieces of skin left around the old carcasses to be found on almost any prairie. He had learned other things too, since the first time he went out, perhaps enough for now.

As he moved southward Elk was torn between two plans. He wanted to get to the Comanches and their fine large horses that came from the Texas and Mexican whites — even more dangerous now that some Comanches had been killed with the Kiowas. Or he might go after mustangs around the remote water holes far from the paths of the migrating buffaloes and so also far from the Indian trails.

Horsecatcher had reminded him of one thing that must always sit upon his heart as the chill of winter sits on the high mountains of summer snow. "Your parents have lost one good son. Would you have their last one taken from them too?"

So Elk turned his face from the Comanche villages and cut across a dry region, carrying his little waterskin, seeking out a place that Horsecatcher had described, one with a string of water holes that would be shrinking and briny now, the spring that fed them only a little running thread. Nothing except horses seemed to find the place — horses, tarantulas, and rattlesnakes. Elk had his hunting bow with him, but mostly he must eat the scarce wild fruits, the prairie peas, the turnips and other roots, perhaps late bird eggs, and even grass. It was becoming increasingly hard for him to kill the gentle rabbit that hopped such a trusting little distance from his moccasins, or the birds whose flushing and cries had saved both the Arrow woman and the Elk.

The young Cheyenne walked for five days, watching for horses and their sign, the narrow paths and the scattered droppings, with perhaps one of the piles of horse manure that the stallions sometimes built on rises, as challenges to others, Horsecatcher thought. Elk watched for other sign too, not forgetting his first time out alone, a little

93

over a year ago, when he was caught by Cheyennes. Now he realized that the one who wanted no fighting must be even more careful, more vigilant.

He traveled so long that his weary legs told him he must have missed the directions Horsecatcher had marked out in the dust with a spear of grass. Surely there was no life on all this parched and empty plain. Then at last he saw a buzzard circling. Something dead or dying, and that was more than he had seen for a whole day over the heated earth. There was a gradual appearance of grass too, and a faint horse trail that led to a low rise. From there he could see a grassed little valley to his left, but perhaps unwatered because the main trail led toward some low bluffs in the west. As Elk followed, it grew plainer, past a gray stretch that was a marsh in the early summers, and beyond that a shrunken water hole at the foot of a brushy draw where the spring must head.

Elk stopped in the shade of a little bank to study the place he planned to haunt for a moon's time, even several if necessary, to get the good horses that Catcher had described, and to tame them enough to get them home. As he watched, a few horses, ten or twelve, came in to the hazy, shimmering bit of water — the horses too far to see the color, and when the air moved it brought a smell of carrion, — buzzard meat, a horse off on a rise, Elk saw, probably killed by lightning.

After a while the young Indian felt he understood the land and that there was perhaps no sign of enemies. He slipped out far around to come in over the head of the draw where the water seemed to start. By then the horses were grazing outward, good horses, but all grays, bays, and sorrels — not the bunch he had come so far to find. But there were tracks of more than one little herd. He could wait.

When the horses were gone, Elk climbed down over the

94

rotten sandstone rim around the top of the draw, moving carefully, with the smell of rattlesnake habitation plain in the broken rock. On the way down the steep slope he had to move aside for a skunk that walked soberly along a narrow ledge, scarcely looking up at the scent of man. There was a little gurgle of water where two small streams of it fell like icicles from a wet shelf of stone and rippled down a steep, rocky groove to a boggy slope and out into the water hole. Most of the hole was clean for all its wide dried and cracking margins. Evidently few creatures except horses came to stir the water here. There was no sign of buffalo, javelina, or even mud hen or duck, although tracks of a doe and her fawn had dried in the soft earth around the willows and a little box elder tree, and a quail whistled on the bluff.

"Ah-h-h!" the young Cheyenne said to himself as he stooped to cup his hand to the water, beautiful, clear cold water. Here he would make his home, without fire or any of the things of man except the inescapable smell until the horses knew him, and if the smell remained enemy to them even in this far place, perhaps the little pack of salt he carried on his back would help them forget.

It was a fine place, with the sky cupped about his shoulders as comfortably as a fine new trader blanket. Yet somehow by sunset he was lonesome, and once he almost started back.

8

*T*HE NEXT DAY was very hot and the horses came to water early. Young Elk watched them string in over the little rise, the leader a bay mare with the longest mane he had ever seen. Hanging to her knees in a black falling, it lifted as she began to trot and blew back in a dark streaming when the smell of water drew her into a gallop. But she stopped short before she reached the hole, her head up, the mane flying about her suspicious head in a great cloud. In the cross wind she got no direct man smell, and so she edged toward the water, the other horses close about her, fifteen in all — five of them the color of new-tanned buckskin, with black mane and tail, the back and legs dark-striped, the young stallion fine-breasted, with a long swinging step.

"If you must remain cool in a fight, ride a horse dun-yellow as the coyote; or travel far, ride such a one. If you must run beyond all horse endurance, then it must be not on a horse, but on that yellow wind, the dun," Horse-catcher once told Elk. Here there were five of them, young, agile, graceful as mountain lions and as dangerous — more so, for who would try to catch a lion alive?

It was Horsecatcher's story of these buckskin-colored horses that had drawn him here. He had told Elk how it would be, and what could be expected. " Other things will happen, my son," the old man said thoughtfully, "things my eyes do not see now. These you must face as you can, and from them we will see how well you have chosen your path. The bird that lives with horses will not fail you if your ears are opened."

And it was true that even here the black bird rode the withers of the two older mares, and sometimes of a curly-maned buckskin colt with a stubborn nose that turned under.

"Become a horse in thought and everything," Horse-catcher had said, and so Elk only looked from far off now, as he thought a strange horse here might. After the herd had watered, rolled in the dust, and wandered away to graze, he worked at the Catcher's advice. He began with the most conspicuous man-thing first — the smell. He dug up a fat yucca root, peeled the brown skin back a half finger's length, and scrubbed the smell from his clothing with the soapy brush this made while he bathed in the farther, the scummy end of the little lake with its stale-water smell. Then he dried in the sun on a sandy spot where the horses had rolled. He built no fire, ate only berries, puffballs, the thick roots of the arrowhead, and rushes, grass seeds, and mints. Otherwise he sat in the scrubby brush downwind from the water, unmoving, watching as the horses came to drink, trying to run beside them in imagination, paw the water, roll in the sand.

The lead mare was still nervous. She always stood off, working her head up and down, her nostrils wide, trying to locate, to identify her uneasiness. Once she snorted and whirled to gallop away, making a great half circle back toward the water, the only sweet water for many miles.

As Horsecatcher predicted, the little herd always finally drank and even rested, but a little farther out now than was usual. But gradually there seemed less uneasiness, until at the end of seven, eight days they came direct as ever to drink, and that night Young Elk felt so good he could hardly sleep. He thought of his family, his sister, Horse-catcher and his wife, but mostly of Red Sleeve, thinking man-thoughts of her, knowing too that there were all the young warriors with coups and honors around, the many new honors from the fight with the Kiowas. The offer of any one of them might be accepted any day, and even though the courtship of a girl like the Sleeve must be a thing of some years, an acceptance was a promise not easily broken.

Once Elk wanted to jump up and start home as fast as his moccasins could carry him over the miles of scattered sage and cactus. But what had he to offer — still called by his boyhood nickname as the son of a man called Elk River? True, his father had sung the name of Kiowa Killer through the village for him, but everyone thought of him as Young Elk, the little son of the Elk.

It was very hard to live here, with very little for a man to eat unless he killed. The berries were soon gone, and while Elk dug roots, there seemed only the dry, unnourishing ones left. He woke hungry in the nights, wishing it were day so he could hunt. Yet in the morning he pushed this from his mind. Perhaps he would have to give up these herds anyway, for time passed and he had no plan. Then one day the horses came stringing along a little late, with one of the mares and the stallion lagging far behind. They had barely settled to their rest, stomping flies around the ragged little willows, when all the heads went up together. Running fast down the narrow, worn trail came a lone horse, a blue-roan, a young stallion looking for a herd. He stopped at the mound of droppings to sniff and then came on faster, tail up, neck bowed, came galloping heavy and hard.

The two younger colts drew close to their mothers in

alarm, the yearlings scattered but looking back curiously. The buckskin stallion stood high, small dark ears up. He gave an angry squeal and, with his head out, he gathered his mares back into an eager but watchful little bunch.. Then, whirling, he kicked up dirt in spurts as he ran out to meet the challenger.

The young blue stopped, sidled off, but the dun bared his teeth and went for him, struck him straight on. The young stallion was ready and they came together, fore-hoofs up like panthers meeting, sparring for the opening. The dun cut in first, his long teeth slashing a red streak in the blue shoulder. The younger took it and whirled to kick in under the dun's flank, lifting the hindquarters, bringing a scream of pain and fury. The dun turned upon the blue, cutting his sharp forehoofs into the shoulders and back, almost beating him down, but the blue-roan slipped side-ways and came up to ward off the attack, snaking in with his sharp teeth, his jaws snapping on the dun's ears, his cheek, his throat as the herd stallion cut the skin and flesh from the blue with his iron-sharp hoofs. They whirled, kicked, one slipping down in the loose, torn earth, the other upon him but not fast enough, not before he was up and running. They fought and ran, first one and then the other, each time the fleeing one whirling upon the pursuer, then the fierce climb up, up on hind legs, each trying to get his striking hoofs above the other's, the crack of hoof on hoof, of teeth meeting teeth, with wild screams of rage and pain that filled the little valley, and between the screams the hoarse, laboring, searing pantings.

It was the wildest, fiercest battle Young Elk ever saw, with the air full of dust and flying earth, the horses cut and torn, covered with dirt, blood dripping. Elk realized that he could run in and perhaps rope a foot of either and drive the other off, but it would be all he caught, only the one, and this time he wasn't after one horse but at least the five buckskins, stallion and all.

So the young Indian did not uncoil his rope from his waist, but waited, ready, almost as the mares waited, curiously milling a little among themselves as their future was decided. The yearling stallions moved closer, watchful, eager, perhaps sensing their turn to come someday.

Gradually the battle slowed, the swift hoofs of the dun still cutting the blue but with less lightning in them, the blue's attacks less swift too, but his teeth still seeking, seeking, and when the dun faltered one moment, the blue slashed out again, missed, and then drove in once more and clamped his jaws on the bloody, sweat-slippery throat of the enemy, on the jugular vein, the windpipe.

The dun was suddenly shrunken, trying to shake the blue loose, to run and to tear loose. Then, as he began to wheeze for breath, he gathered his power together and threw himself as high as he could with the clamped jaw and the weight of the young horse dragging at him. He drove his hoofs against the shoulders of the blue, tearing the flesh in strips as he came down. He lashed at the blue's withers, and rocked him on his struggling feet until they went over together, shaking the earth, their hoofs tearing at each other like clawing panthers. But they were slowing, tiring, the dun's whistling breath like a blizzard wind; the blue, battered and shaken like a bundle of old hides, hung to the dun's throat as his belly was raked and ripped until he had to scream his pain and loose the hold of his jaws.

Struggling to his feet, the young stallion slunk away, limping, worn. He was overtaken by the laboring buckskin, kicked, struck once more — weakly, but the inexperienced young blue took it all with lowered head. It was only an attack for show now. Actually the dun seemed glad to let him go, and slowly started back to what was still his herd, blood streaming in red rivulets through the dust caked over him, and in a thicker flow at the throat

100

wound. The curious mares moved back a little from the smell of the blood, from the injured, as animals naturally do. They nickered their foolish colts back too, looking toward their stallion as his legs suddenly crumpled under him and he went down flat. The blue challenger did not look back to see the easy victory he could take now, but limped on over the little rise.

Young Elk was still trembling from the battle he had seen. But soon he was the young horsecatcher again. The blue stallion must have been very badly hurt and would probably be dead by morning or so stiff that he could be roped easily and hobbled. After that it would be up to the Elk. He looked off to the buckskin, lying flat. Now was certainly the time for another stallion to come running in, neck bowed, prancing, but somehow it didn't occur to the young Indian to add his rope to the injuries laid upon the dun by the vanquished blue.

Elk had to dig a few roots to quiet his empty stomach, and decided to build a bit of fire to roast them, now that he had one horse, if the dun lived. But Elk still felt gaunt as a hungry coyote and he slept uneasily that night, with a curious dreaming, a confusion of horses, white horses, and man, with something of the battle of the stallions here, and a feast and dancing in the village at home, with Red Sleeve drawing him along into the circle, going very fast, until it seemed he was very tall, the height of two men, and there was no one with him but Red Sleeve, soft-eyed and still modest.

When he awoke there was a singing in his breast for all his hunger, and then Elk discovered it was some blackbirds along the water and one of the sweet-singing birds that mocked them sitting above the brush patch where Elk had slept, all acting as though there were no enemy man around anywhere.

Elk rose quickly, drank at the finger of cold water falling

101

from the rock, and remembered the day before and the fight of the stallions. He glanced out over the little flat, the earth torn by the struggle, and saw that the buckskin was just where he went down yesterday. Elk approached him cautiously. The horse struggled to his feet, but took only a few stiff and awkward steps and let himself down again, his hindquarters weakening. He struggled only a little when the young Indian threw a rope hobble on his fore-legs, but as Elk was tying them he looked to where the blue stallion had come over the rise yesterday. It was dangerous to leave the dun so helplessly hobbled, although he was almost as helpless free.

Then the young Cheyenne brought clean water from the spring in his skin bag, but the horse refused to drink, so he made a little rawhide-lined water hole and went to sit behind him, downwind, patient. Several times the horse looked back toward the youth. Finally he reached out uncertainly to the water and drew back from the man smell, but after a while he drank, clear down to the bottom, and when Elk came to see, there was no wet spot on the deeply cut throat, no sign of water leaking from it, and no wheeze of escaping breath, although blood began to ooze a little when the horse moved.

It was a grieving thing to see these hurts, these woundings. His skin, which had been a dun rich as sunlight on fall bunch grass, was torn and scarred and swollen so that barely one spot the size of the palm remained sound. Making his soft, friendly murmurings, Elk went over all of these, belly and all, touching them gently with the flat of his hand. At first the horse shied from this touch, snorting, perhaps more from fear than the pain, but he quieted and closed his torn eyelids while the Elk rubbed the velvety ear root, careful not to touch the tears and cuts or to press anywhere. He bent to listen at the swollen throat wound again to reassure himself that the windpipe was not broken, wishing that Horsecatcher were here with his knowledge, his good horse medicine ways. If the yellow one here didn't die and Elk got him home, it would be a very good sign of luck from the Great Powers.

Elk settled himself beside the stallion's black nose, making his soft little coaxing sounds, touching the shivering skin gently, letting the horse learn the man smell. Before the herd came in to water he left to hunt more roots and then to sit in the shady bushes to watch them trail in. The lead mare was very suspicious, waiting a long time to test the hot wind as the others came up about her. The thirst of the heat drove another mare to start ahead, but the leader warned her back with a threat and trotted out, the chastized one following behind with lowered head. So they came, swinging out around the stallion, the natural animal reluctance to go near another in injury as strong as in birth, mating, sickness, or death.

Elk expected to see the blue stallion come limping along behind, driven in by his need for water but keeping his proper distance and position now. When he didn't appear, the Indian turned his eyes to the light windy sky for buzzards or perhaps even an eagle circling over east. But it was high and empty.

He decided to go over that way when the horses were gone, and then suddenly he forgot all about the blue-roan. The dun stallion was struggling up, awkward from his injuries and the binding of his legs. He sat on his haunches awhile, striking and snapping at the hobbles. It was all Elk could do to hold himself from running out to quiet the wild horse, afraid that the dun in his fright would fly into a terrified fury, perhaps break a leg or his neck in the frantic fighting against the ties that held his feet.

But the horse seemed to treat the hobbles as one more crippling result of his fight, and, instead of struggling long against them, he tested the extent of his freedom as well as he could and then started for the lake, awkwardly lifting his two forelegs together. He drank a little, slowly, swished the surface scum back with his nose, and drank again. Then he moved out to find a scattered mouthful of grass here and there on his way over the rise to the range. Elk wished he could feed him here, not need to let him go into the great danger from enemies, animal and man. But the flat around the water hole was grazed very bare.

By evening the horse was at the top of the rise, golden once more in the last rays of sun that struck him as he rested a moment and then went down the other side. Young Elk was happy. Unless something happened that he couldn't manage, or enemies or another stallion came — a young stallion that wasn't afraid of the man smell of the hobbles — he might have a fine five-year-old stud for his father's herd.

Or perhaps this one should go to Horsecatcher, although he wished the dun might be tied beside the lodge of Red Sleeve as evidence that he, Young Elk, was worth accepting as a son by her family, a son to be forever a worthy member of his wife's people.

Heat lightning helped the empty belly to keep Young Elk awake that night, with occasional crashing bolts that ripped the sky and the prairie. Several times he climbed to the top of the canyon to look over the lightning-split little flat, hoping that the rain would pass around, as it plainly did most of the time. A rain would fill the baked water holes in the lower valley and over where the grass grew. Then he couldn't hope to capture the rest of the duns until next summer. He thought about making a little weather medicine and put the thought aside. "Good medicine is made when it's for the people," the wise men of his tribe always said, men like Elk River, Owl, and Ridge Tree, men who lived good lives this way.

By dawn no more than a scattered spatter of great drops had fallen under the glare of the heat lightning, and wrapped themselves in gray dust almost as soon as they fell. Elk thought about the blue stallion, afraid that, if still alive, he would recover enough to kill the hobbled dun, even though he was too weak or afraid yesterday to come for water.

At dawn Elk started up over the ridge to see. The horses were in a little cluster about a mile off. He swung far around behind them, and as the sun rose he came over a low knoll not far away. For a moment his heart seemed to stop, and guilt flooded over him. There was the blue, grazing easily with the rest, the dun stallion nowhere in sight.

9

*Y*OUNG ELK grieved for his fine buckskin stallion, probably dead somewhere, dead of his wounds or killed by the untrammeled blue-roan. But there was deep gauntness in the young Indian's belly, and first he had to look for something to eat, wondering if he might not feel better, more like the brightness of the sun all about him, if he got a little meat. But for that he must kill a rabbit or a young duck, perhaps, or one of the sage hens that came to the water and stood looking at Elk so curiously, their broad silvery breasts gleaming in the early sun.

He finally decided to kill a hen, and went far off from the water hole so nothing of death would be brought around there. With a plump young sage hen he settled into a little dry washout on the flat tableland, where no sharp-nosed enemy could sneak upon the smell of smoke unnoticed. Here Elk built a little nest of roasting coals from gnarled sagebrush. He ate like a starved man, and felt comforted and a little ashamed.

Afterward he found a few prairie turnips and dug them, saving two for later. It was midafternoon when he started back to the water hole, cutting across some broken knobs, and was close to a horse in the shadows before he realized it — a horse that faded into the yellowish breaks, the stallion that was dun as a summer coyote. Elk stopped and waited until the horse moved, still hobbled, the rawhide ties holding. Easily, unhurried, and like a friend, he walked toward the stallion, but the horse moved away, hopping sideways, and Elk did not follow because he would not be an enemy now, not a pursuer. Instead, he squatted down and poured a little salt from the pouch at his belt upon a clean, hard-packed spot and waited, making the same little coaxing noises of all the hours he had sat beside the dun after the fight. Drawn by the native mustang curiosity that Horsecatcher stressed so much, the stallion came nearer, circling awkwardly to get the smell of the man, and, by his snorting, remind Elk that he had eaten meat, the scent of the enemy.

But gradually the dun reached his neck out, moving his head cautiously to sniff the earth and the air. He did this stiffly, painfully, the wounding on the throat swollen large as a buffalo bladder of meat, and as dark, with pus stringing from it, and fly-blown. Elk managed to hold himself quiet while the horse sniffed and jumped back, snorting. Finally he edged up to the salt, bent to it, licked it eagerly. Slowly the Elk's hand went out to the torn, ragged jaw and crept to the velvety trough underneath. The dun turned his head away a moment but let the hand follow and move up under the ragged, dirty mane, let the Indian breathe into his nostrils, making himself familiar. It took patience, but before sunset Elk had a rope about the horse's nose and up over the ears instead of around the swollen neck. Then he went all over the torn hide with a gentle touch, wondering what he should do. The dun must have grass, and yet Elk couldn't turn him loose without hobbles, and certainly not hobbled, to be killed by the blue or any other roving, herd-hunting stallion, or picked up by passing Kiowas.

The Elk looked at the torn hide, all scabbed over against dirt and flies except the deep and inflamed throat wound. He wished Horsecatcher could be here to say what must be done, what herb brew might cure this. But the horse seemed less sick now than before, and when the salt was gone, he started off to the water hole, Elk letting the rope out, trailing behind, stopping whenever the dun stopped to crop bits of stray grass. At the water he drank deeply and then settled down for the night. The Elk stayed beside him, the rope in his hand, and looked at the clear star paths across the sky, trying to plan the next day. Once he smelled a whiff of the raw, greenish smell of a rattlesnake, like the cucumbers he had seen in the garden at Bent's Fort. He knew that some of the snakes were shedding their skins, from the eyes too, and so were very much afraid and angered that they could not see. Elk held himself still and the smell did not come again.

Toward morning the stallion snorted and rose, stumbling in the hobbles. Elk slackened the rope so he could walk farther away, and together they went awkwardly up the trail toward the grassy little flat, the lithe, easy-walking young Indian behind the hobbled horse. Elk hoped they wouldn't meet the herd coming to water. When they got to the top of the little ridge he saw the horses still feeding below them, the big blue alert, head raised, looking. Once he ran a ways and then circled around until he got the man smell and stopped, whirled, and was gone, his smoky mane flying.

Elk felt easier. For a while at least he could hold the blue off, but later — he must plan carefully for later.

After the dun had fed awhile, Elk began serious work with him. At first he plunged away, twice jerking the lightly held rope out of the Indian's hand. But he couldn't escape the swift feet, the hand always back at the dragging rope, and finally he quieted again to the coaxing, wordless sounds, the gentle hand all over him. So the Elk worked until the sun burned hot down upon them and the horse could be drawn from one grass plot to another by a pull forward on the rope and the mane.

Gradually Elk put weight on the dark-lined back of the buckskin, even though it was still scabbed and sore. First his hand pushed down a little, then he laid his arm across it, and finally he leaned heavily over the horse, lifting his feet a moment. The horse plunged sideways at the unaccustomed weight, so Elk went all over him again and let the uneasy nostrils sniff him carefully, rolling a testing breath upon him. Then Elk went around to the right and pressed on ribs and spine while the horse turned his head to watch, the great dark eyes burning with suspicious fire. Suddenly Elk leaned over the back again, clear over, running his hands along the belly on the far side, holding to the mane until the struggling horse quieted a little. Then easily, confidently, Elk put a leg over the back and was astride the dun, a hand secure in the root of the mane.

The startled horse stood a moment, and then he jerked his head down to buck, but the hobbles threw him, Elk slipping off as he went down, and back before the dun was on his feet again. Talking to the horse, Elk urged him ahead by pushing with the heels of his hands on the withers and swinging his weight forward. The stallion took one step, then another, lifting his hobbled feet together, carefully.

Finally Elk slipped off, patted and rubbed the healing nose, and put a couple of prairie turnips into the corner of the horse's mouth, watching him chew them slowly. For the present Elk was well satisfied, but he must manage to protect the dun, and then there were the others besides the duns to catch, particularly the blue, who would be a fine hunting horse after the quieting medicine thong that Horsecatcher had shown him how to make.

Toward evening the dun seemed thirsty, and Elk rode him in. There he washed some of the maggots from the

109

swollen throat wound with a thin lather made from the yucca, the soapweed, roots and watched the bird that lives with horses eat them. He spread ashes mixed with the fat from the sage hen over the wounds on the withers and along the back to keep the gathering magpies off. He had seen these birds drive sore-backed horses crazy, clinging to their running, bucking backs as they tore at the wounds, sometimes digging so deep into the kidney region that the poor animals died.

But most of the time Elk worked to teach his new horse to lead, to respond to knee pressure, turn, start, stop. The Indian was gentle but firm, and the coyote-dun learned very fast on all but following the pull of the rope. A loop around the nose discouraged jerking back because it shut off his wind, and by night it seemed safe to picket the horse to a tree while Elk slept nearby, curled up under the soft light of the growing moon.

In the morning the dun stallion made his first friendly move toward the young Indian, almost as though he understood the cause of his easing wounds. Elk had come back from the spring with a big handful of green grass he pulled under the rocks. The stallion sniffed it and then rubbed his nose against Elk's arm. Finally he took a mouthful and munched it a little awkwardly, not yet used to the jaw rope.

Elk rode him over to graze with the hobble on only one leg now, so the dun could walk, even run, freely, but with the rope end in his hand the rider could throw the horse if he broke to go wild or to attack the blue, who trumpeted his challenge but was still afraid of this horse-man creature.

Elk wondered now at his foolishness when he started out to catch the duns. Even with the luck of the stallion fight he had no plans. True, the herd could be weakened by thirst as he had caught the Bear Colt, except that these were many and strong horses. He remembered that Horse-

110

catcher said there were things Elk must work out for himself, things the old man's eyes could not foresee. On the dun, but without much hope, Elk started to keep the horses from water, holding them in the grazing valley as long as he could. But another little herd came in from the south, and with this encouragement and the drive of thirst, the lead mare grew bolder. At the ridge, with her mane and tail a streaming of black, she whirled and went around the dun one way while her followers ran the other. Elk's stallion, content with his usual place behind the herd, even behind the threatening blue now, had to be kicked and whipped to head off the mares. At this first punishment he had ever felt, he stretched out like a wolf and passed all the other horses, even the lead mare. At the water hole Elk drew him up and hoped, by the man smell, to keep the little herd away. They did stop, looking, standing in an uneasy row, the colts beside the mares, all taut, heads up, manes blowing.

But Elk knew the time would come when thirst would drive them against every fear, even the wild bay mare and surely the blue stallion. By then he hoped the blue would be so weak that the dun could conquer more easily, if it came to a struggle, a driving out, but that he hoped to avoid now. He wished Horsecatcher were here to help him. Or the very good warrior Two Wolves. Together they could do anything. But now the brother lay in the burial rocks down in Kiowa country, where the first light of the eastern sun struck.

Elk tried to imagine how it would be at home if he could return with at least the five duns, the fine stallion all healed and prancing. Certainly Red Sleeve would stop a moment to talk inside his blanket then, and draw him into the dance after the feast his father would surely make. Then he would go down to sit beside the bones of his brother awhile — on the way to visit with the Comanches, even though they would count him their enemy, their escaped captive. This going to the Comanches he must manage, if only to see the maidens who could capture wild horses so well. He must see whether it was possible for the sisters to do the difficult things that were told.

But now the horses here were sneaking past him toward the water, past the foolish dreamer that Young Elk was. He whooped and drove them back. They went, but reluctantly, and as the moon climbed and showed the horses pushing in, Elk knew he had to do something stronger. He could gather enough sagebrush and other dead wood for little fires for one night, but that must be saved for an emergency. He would surely tire without sleep, and the moon might be clouded so he could not see the horses sneak up. For tonight he left his barefoot tracks in the mud around the water hole, and kept a bit of fire going. Even so, he had to run around the water several times more as the eyes reflecting the little fire drew very near.

In the morning the weary youth hazed the reluctant horses over to their range, but he had trouble holding them there long enough to let the dun feed, and he knew that tomorrow it would be hopeless. He was worn and hungry and weak with thinking of what was ahead of him. He wished he had tried to get someone to come along. Still, this was the test, as Horsecatcher had said. "It is very dangerous, and very hard — " he had warned. So far Elk had seen little danger, except from the lightning-fast hoofs of the dun, or the rattlesnakes he smelled, and, of course, from the gaunt belly of starvation if he would not kill food. But there was another danger that Horsecatcher warned about — the thin old war trail against the Utes, but perhaps not used more than once or twice a year by the southern tribes.

When the noon sun drew the shadows in about the feet, Elk had to race the herd to the lake. The dun beat them, drove them back, the mares with colts made very sly by their need, their desperation. The blue stallion tried to slip past very close, bluffing the man smell, but the dun snaked his head out and gave the blue a vicious nip as he cut in ahead of him, and Elk brought his whip down hard on the blue rump.

Still, Elk knew this was about the last time he could hold the herd back, and alone he couldn't make anything of their weakness, couldn't walk or ride more than one of them down, and that much he had done his first time out, afoot. He had to try to get a little sleep now, probably his last before he gave up. With his loop ready, and the dun's jaw rope over his arm, he dozed a little, and was awakened almost at once, it seemed, by a shrill crying. The bay mare was almost to the water and the bird that sat the sleeping dun's back was squawking loudly.

Weary, hopeless, Elk drove the herd away once more, still not able to get to the blue with his rope. Then suddenly he had an idea. One of the more inquisitive and daring of the yearlings had climbed up to the top of the box canyon, drawn by the smell of the spring. Elk let her go, and then had to run, whooping and waving his arms. She had her head stretched down over the sandstone outcroppings, and in a moment she would have been over them and sliding the broken slope to water.

Now Elk laughed aloud at his foolishness. He had been worrying about wearing out the horses through thirst before they played him out for sleep, and here was the solution, the plan, right before his eyes. He hobbled the dun and then settled to sleep in the shade of the little willows, keeping himself awake only long enough to watch the lead mare bring the rest running in to the water. Most of them waded far out as though they would have more water sooner that way, as though they must hold it so none could take it away.

In the morning Elk climbed up to where the yearling almost went over yesterday. Pounding with loose rocks, he broke a path through the rotten sandstone that rimmed the little box draw, broke it down enough so that not even the colts would have much trouble getting over the outcropping, to slip and slide down to the spring pocket. Then he stopped to roast some roots from the grassy valley over east, drank at the spring, and climbed up to sit leaning against the rock bank, and felt as powerful as a great wind that could bend the trees and drive the storm clouds racing.

Perhaps he dozed a little, for suddenly he realized he smelled the cucumber odor of a rattlesnake, but very strong this time, so strong he knew the snake must be very large and very close to him, perhaps coming out of the rocks behind his leaning back — silent, shedding the skin and rattles and very dangerous. This time the smell did not go away, and so he waited, holding himself motionless, stopping even the rise and fall of his breathing until it seemed everything was already going dark as death, as though he had been bitten in his sleep. When it seemed he could not hold himself but must jump, even though the move would bring the swift fangs, he heard a soft dry stirring, and a great flat, arrow-shaped head appeared where he could see it with the corner of his eye. The snake crept slowly past his naked elbow, the ragged skin loosening about the head and rustling softly like willow leaves drying with fall. The rattler moved slowly, clumsily, the length of Elk's arm and hand, turning, twisting this way and that in its blindness, the body thick as Elk's arm, the black diamonds of it glossy where the old skin was tearing off. Once the snake touched Elk's leg and snapped back into a half coil, ready to strike at any movement. But Elk held himself as still as the earth, and the snake lengthened out again and went sliding down and around his moccasin.

114

Now suddenly Elk couldn't hold himself. He sprang up, grabbed a heavy rock in both hands. The snake snapped into a great pile of coils at the first movement, the broad and terrible head turned toward him, wavering, catching the sense of the enemy. Elk sent the stone crashing upon the snake. The head dodged and struck the stone, mouth open, the fangs half as long as the Elk's little finger. Then, too swift for the eye, the snake straightened out and raced toward the rocky shelf. Elk grabbed up more stones, threw them, more and more. One hit, then another. The snake, back broken, struck out at them again and again, its great mouth snapping open. Then it turned upon the rock that held the broken back, and upon its own unmoving length beyond. Elk hurled more and more rocks and stones upon the writhing, flattening coils until the snake was finally dead, only the tail still moving.

Afterward the young Cheyenne held his sickened stomach and was ashamed, for toward the last all the snake had tried to do was shield its broad head under the rocks that had destroyed its power to move.

Afterward, with his knife, Elk snapped off what was left of the fangs, to avoid accidental punctures from the head that still tried to strike again as soon as it was freed. Then he skinned the snake and stretched the hide with willow withes to dry. It would make a fine cover for the arrows of one of his friends, or for the pipe of Elk River. The young Indian roasted a length of the flesh, white as frog legs, and ate it with relish on top of his meal of roots, which had been truly poor fare. Besides, when is the young Indian ever full?

All this time Elk planned his mustang pen. First he must take the dun over to grass, and when he returned he would start planning how to shut off the little box canyon at the bottom. With luck he might trap the whole herd.

115

10

THE LITTLE mustang pen was done, the foot of the narrow little canyon filled higher than Elk's arm could reach, with gaps in the rock layers at the bottom to let the threads of spring water through. On top of these layers Elk had piled brush interwoven with more rocks and topped by three small willow trees cut down with all their branches and weighted into place with rock.

By now the dun was gentle and reliable so long as no mare drew him, and for those times there were still the hobbles. Once more Elk started turning the horses from the water hole, but he let them climb up the bluff to look down over the rocky canyon wall to the fine smell of fresh cold water. By evening the lead mare had gone over the rim rock and down the slide on her haunches, slipping and tumbling, but getting up unhurt to drink deep from the clear little spring pool, turning her eyes uneasily toward the rough wall that was new below her, but still drinking. Then she went to it, looking up to the top and down along the bottom, snorting at the strong enemy smell, sniffing at the holes for the water, but there was no place to see through or to get a nose over.

By now others had followed her, going down the smoothening slide, or snorting and faunching around uneasily at the top until the rocky rim crumbled off in dust

116

under their sharp hoofs and they slid and rolled down too. Those below were milling around against Elk's wall even though he stood nearby to see if it would hold, to add the fear of man to the brush and rock. The trapped mustangs crowded against it, but shied off too, and it seemed that so long as the bottom of the boxy little pen didn't fill in too much with loose dirt the horses could be held. Finally there was only one horse left outside, a frightened colt, plunging back and forth, whinnying, afraid of the steep drop.

Young Elk slept fitfully that night, but in the morning all the horses except the dun picketed at his hand and the one colt were still inside. Their milling around had churned the ground down against Elk's pen wall into mud, which might grow high enough for the lead mare to get her wily mustang nose over. When she did she would be gone, and the rest after her. So, before sunrise, Elk was inside roping the horses. It was easy enough for him now, but not so easy to keep from being run over in the narrow pen while he tied the hobbles on. Elk started with the blue-roan first. The young stallion, sensing his danger, hid his head behind the rest, plunging back and forth in the tight, rocky little place, throwing mud, churning the little marshy slope to bedrock. But Elk finally footed him with a little loop, brought him down in a hard, ground-rocking fall, and, with rawhide hobbles secure, let him up. He took the bay lead mare next, and after that the duns and the rest were easier, although there was still the danger of the horses jamming through his wall or of getting himself kicked or run over, with no one around to save an injured Indian, or free the trapped horses if he died. He wished he could have held the horses a couple of days, gentled them before tying their feet, but there was danger that desperation would help them get out or that enemies might come riding the old trail to the Ute country.

By night Young Elk had all but the colts hobbled. His knee and both shoulders were sprained and skinned to bleeding, and one of his ears was torn half off by the lead mare when she jerked her head loose. But the young Indian had tied it down right away with his braids wrapped tightly around his head, one over his forehead, the other over the top and down under his chin. After resting a little, Elk still had the strength to break down his wall of rocks and brush to let the horses out into the late evening light. It was sad to see the herd, so proud a few hours before, with fire in their eyes, their manes blowing beautiful and free, now move out stiffly, awkwardly, lifting the forefeet together, heads down, into the shadowed valley.

Next morning Young Elk walked among them as they struggled over the rise to their range letting them learn the smell of him, hear his friendly voice, his easy familiarity with their dun stallion, leg-free and following the rope as readily as any village horse. He had to be kept beyond kicking distance from most of the mares and away from the blue stallion, but otherwise it was easy enough. Even the loose colts were getting curious, coming to sniff the young Indian, and then whirling to run and kick their heels. It was a happiness to be walking so among these horses, particularly among the fine coyote-duns, but he knew there was much trouble ahead — to get them home, particularly when the big bay mare suddenly stopped to fight the hobbles, going for them as furiously as for an attacking mountain lion. She tried to kick forward at the rawhide holding her forelegs, slashed at it with her teeth as she would at a clinging yellow lion. Elk ran in as close as he dared and tried to soothe her with his gentle sounds and with firm commands, but the fiery mare reared away from him and went down over her head. Struggling to her feet, she got away to attack the hobbles once more with her powerful teeth, until she threw herself again. This

118

time Elk was on her neck and before he let her up he tied her head back to the root of her tail so she could not bite her hobbles. It was cruel, and yet Elk knew that he must hold this one or perhaps lose the entire little bunch. If they got away he would have to give them up. He hadn't the heart now to recapture this wily herd.

Besides, he must remember the other danger that grew as the season latened, when enemies would cut through this way from their forays against the mountain Indians. It was over a wide dry region, but for men in a hurry it saved at least two sleeps of travel.

By evening the bay mare was following the pull of the jaw rope, and let Elk put his weight over her back. Tomorrow he would teach her to carry him and to guide by knee pressure and side sway, to leave the hunter and the warrior freehanded for bow and lance. Tomorrow too Elk must try to make the gelding band for the blue stallion. He had done this only once, with Horsecatcher there to watch, and on a yearling. He should have green hide for this, but he must try to use a strip of rawhide that he had put to soak two days ago. In the morning he undertook the task of turning the blue into a fast, reliable, and hardy horse for the hunt, the races, and even for war or flight. The blue-roan color was known for speed as the dun was for courage and endurance. When it was done, Elk knew he must watch the drying rawhide band so it did not become tight enough to kill, and yet remained tight enough to cut down the circulation.

Two days later all this quiet time was broken as a willow stick over the knee. He had started the horses back to the water hole through the evening sun. As always, he rode ahead and got off to peer over the little ridge. This time he ducked his head low immediately. There was a twist of smoke rising into the still air at the willows, and nearby a man was watering eleven or twelve horses, ready to take them out for a little grass, perhaps. This was what the Elk had feared. Now he must either pull off all the hobbles and let the horses, all but the dun stallion, go free, or take a chance on letting the enemy Indians get them all. and perhaps him too, for surely they had read the fresh sign of him all around the water hole.

But if they didn't know about this grassy little valley, they might think he had gone. Perhaps he could hide the horses somewhere. He wished now that he had scouted the region as a warrior like his brother, Two Wolves, would have done the first day. Now he would have to be sly as a weasel and as lucky, if he were to get away. The horses were working slowly toward the top of the rise. He had to head them, yet ride so slowly that there would be little noise or shaking of the earth to carry to any ear laid to the ground. The Indians down there must be a Kiowa or Comanche war party going home, and they might hurry off southeastward early in the morning. He had to try to hide the horses somewhere to the west so the Indians wouldn't cross the hobbled tracks. He moved them very slowly through the gathering dusk, riding just below the crests of the little rises himself, until he noticed the horses of the Indians turning their heads to look, several neighing. But this was mustang country and evidently too late to stir the Indians to much scouting, for none came out of the camp to look. Finally the Elk left his slow, jumping little herd and hunted out a shallow but long snake-head draw, with a scattering of sand rock and brush in the bottom. Here was a place, the only place he could hope to find. But it would take all night to get the horses to it, even if the waning moon remained clear. Perhaps he should just start for home on the coyote-dun.

But he couldn't give up the fine little herd, not the fast-

120

blooded blue-roan or the other buckskins, and as he thought of this a bird flew up out of the shadow at his feet and fluttered over the ground as though crippled, making an odd, whirring sound. The Elk had never heard this song, and the nesting season was finished long ago, yet the bird flew like a nesting mother, to toll the enemy away — flew with a wing crippled, no, more like a wing hobbled.

"Ah-h-h," Elk said softly to the bird. "Perhaps you are a sign," and made a gesture of thanks.

It took most of the night to get around behind the spring canyon to the draw. The fresh tracks would show that hobbled horses had come this way, yet perhaps the Indians would not follow the horse trail over the ridge, but would turn eastward along the low sandy path of the dry wash where there might be grass, and water too, for the digging. If they headed northeastward instead, off toward the Cheyenne camps, then the dun stallion would have to carry Elk home with the warning.

At dawn the young Cheyenne was looking down on the horses of the Indians held all night at the water hole, without good grass, so they must be planning to hurry on, either chasing other enemies than a youth with a little herd of horses, or fleeing. Smoke was already rising from near the spring where the mustang trap was so fresh and plain. Although there seemed no women along, there were two pony drags, the kind made for the wounded. And while Elk watched, he missed seeing one of the men until he was almost at the top of the bluff, not an arrow's flight from Elk, hidden in a bunch of yucca and sage. On his belly he looked off northward, probably in the direction that they had come from. He stayed there a long time, and the Elk had to hold himself still, for there was no place to run on the bare table from the Kiowa warrior, a warrior of the people who had so much fresh-shed blood to avenge.

There was no telling how much nearer the Kiowa might come, or even whether he had seen Elk. All the Cheyenne could do was push himself close to the earth, remembering the Arrow Keeper's wife saying, "Earth, we are part of you —" He emptied his mind of all things but this, and lay as unmoving as the ground beneath him for a long, long time. He made his back and head feel like nothing, as though they were not there, and no target any moment for a Kiowa club or spear.

When Elk finally dared lift his head to peer around and over the bank, the Kiowa scout on the ridge was riding in a sign of enemies coming, a little sign, meaning only a few, but coming, and so the party down at the water hole began to ride, the travois poles stirring up dust, the scout following, to stop on the ridge above the little flat where the horses had been, and Elk feared for the tracks of the hobblings. But the scout seemed to ride on, and after a while Elk crept out to look back northward, at a fast moving string of dust — Indian pursuers. He hurried to his horses in the gully to keep them quiet, divert them from whinnying. By the time the sun boiled down hot the pursuing party was gone after the fleeing Kiowas. Elk loosed the hobbles of the dun and rode to a high point. All the burning country was empty, so he drove his horses to water. Then he doubled the gelding band on the blue and changed the hobbles on all the stronger horses to a rawhide tied around the flank and to one forefoot so they could walk easily but would fall at a run. The yearlings and colts he left free.

Now, without waiting for another such scare — with perhaps more parties coming through as more water holes dried up — he started northeast, homeward, moving homeward, moving slowly, looking back and all around. No telling how many other war parties were out.

At first the horses kept trying to turn from his driving,

122

to run, particularly the lead mare, her bay skin glinting golden in the sun, until she threw herself into the dust. The blue had to be driven along, stopping every little while to nip at his binding, lagging, sick. And when Elk was far out on flat ground where no one could hear, he sang a little song to the bird that lives with horses. These wild creatures who chose to live in such a hard, empty place were very cunning, and Young Elk wished for the gift of their ways. True, the horses had gaunted down during the last hard week, fighting the hobbles instead of feeding, and Elk himself felt as though his ribs were as bare as the bleaching carcasses on the prairie, with so little time to find food. Although the horses resisted leaving their usual range, they went, and the way they smelled the earth, lifted their ears, found one easy path and then another, Elk knew that they sensed many things that he could not see.

The young Indian had miles of enemy country to cover, yet he felt very lucky. Not the stallion fight, the rattlesnake, or the Kiowas had touched him. Each time it was steeling himself to wait when he wanted to move, to run; it was making himself take thought, act carefully. Now there were other things to think about too, with the white horse, the White One of the south, coming up in his mind.

Yet as Elk looked over his little herd, with the fine duns and the rest, he sang, "We have horses, little bird, we have the horses for Red Sleeve —"

When he was in country well watched by the Cheyenne warriors against encroaching enemies, Young Elk moved more slowly, letting the horses rest and feed where the summer grasses were fat with seed while he went among them with a taming hand. He might have remained a few more days, but the buffaloes were coming in, and he wanted no tangling of hobbled horses, not even the single hobbles, with a herd of buffaloes.

Then one afternoon a Cheyenne scout caught a flash of Elk's looking-glass signals. Several young men came out to meet him, to help him with the herd. Two were childhood friends who had gone into warrior societies, but now they helped rub the horses to a shining with sand and handfuls of grass and then cut the hobbles so Elk could make a proper entrance. Horsecatcher was out standing at the edge of the village, peering under a bony old hand. "You have done well, my son," he said after he had looked at the herd through a whole pipe's smoking in silence. "Very well," he added when he saw how the gelding had been done.

Now Elk's father came too, and several other men. They walked ahead of the horses as they were driven around the village to show off the golden bay lead mare and her herd of fifteen, one of them plainly a very fast blue, and the five fine coyote-duns, including the stallion stepping proudly, neck bowed, eyes full of fire as he carried his young rider. And all of these had been caught by a youth not yet grown, afoot and alone, one who had been shunned because he would not make war, not even to avenge his brother.

All the women were out before the lodges to look under their shading hands in the evening sun, Elk's mother and sister smiling proudly, already painted and adorned for his safe return. Horsecatcher's wife was there too, and the old Arrow Keeper's wife. Red Sleeve came, to stand alone for the Elk's return, with no young man near.

After the feasting Elk's uncle, Owl of the Bowstrings, made a little speech. "Perhaps our son should start a new society, the Horsecatchers!" he said, laughing a little.

Then they went over to the dancing, people looking after them as they passed, some a little distantly because

124

there was the strangeness of a far place and a long absence about the young Cheyenne, a place that seemed much farther than where he had gone, and an absence much longer than it had been. But one small boy rode his stick horse along beside Elk and his uncle, bucking his heels like a very wild mustang.

Tonight Red Sleeve drew Elk into the dancing the first of all, and the stars had turned very far before he could slip out to the herd to find Bear Colt. A long time he searched for the great white bear patch and suddenly feared that the Colt had been lost, a loss like a second brother. But when Elk sat down and made the short little birdcalls, he heard curious feet come out of a draw, starting, stopping, staying away from him a long while. At last the yearling was there, a grass breath at Elk's ear, a soft nose nibbling at his braids. He turned, caught the young horse around the neck, and ran his hand over the lean, lengthening back in the dusky starlight. Colt had grown very much in the two moons that Elk was gone, and his white bear patch was clear and large, and very warm to the searching palm.

11

*W*HEN Young Elk left, the village was in mourning for Gray Thunder, Keeper of the Sacred Arrows. But now, two moons later, it was moved to a new place clean of sorrow, with a new man made Keeper and the Arrow Lodge set up in its honored place once more. The people were ready to go to Bent's Fort with the winter buffalo robes well tanned, many ornamented with paint, quills, and beading during the idle summer days. These would be traded for powder and lead for the fall hunts, and blankets, flannel, and calico, for coffee and the brown sugar, the sweet lumps that were so good in the bottom of the cup.

Young Elk was busy taming his horses, gentling them, training the blue to race as his nature gentled, increasing his second wind too, until he could leave every other horse of the village far behind in the dust. "Now you have a horse to overtake the wild one when there is no time for other ways," Old Horsecatcher said in satisfaction.

The lead mare with the cloud of dark mane and tail, her bay coat gleaming like gold in the sunlight, Elk offered to his teacher. The old Cheyenne looked at her a long, long time, with his faded eyes alight, but even so he made the denying motion. He would accept the rattlesnake skin for his ceremonial pipe, but the fine mare Elk must keep to

126

head his own herd, which he would join to the horses of his wife's family someday — the young husband's offering to the herds of the family welcoming him, to protect and help and love as a son, a brother and nephew.

But Young Elk, thinking of Red Sleeve, felt the heat of embarrassment run up his face, and he tried to busy himself putting the mare down into the grass as though they were hiding in a buffalo wallow from a sharp-eyed foe. Then the mare was taken to his father's herd, along with the fine duns and the blue. The rest were mostly given to needy people who had lost their young men and their horses in the fights with the Kiowas, and in this it was seen that Young Elk had the ways of his father and grandfathers, good chiefs who saw that their people did not want for anything.

While Elk worked, he put the fat on his ribs that his mother said he needed as she added extra meat to the kettle and to his big horn spoon passed to him beside the fire. She said this to Elk's sister or to anyone who was there, and with a smiling face, letting her son see her concern of the two months he was away, yet, as a good Cheyenne mother, doing and saying nothing to soften, to weaken his resolution.

After a little dancing over Elk's horse capture, not a big warrior dance but some dancing, he was invited to visit the Bowstrings. They wished him to join them in honor of his brother killed by the Kiowas.

"But I cannot go on the warpath," Young Elk said, still the shamed boy before these brave men.

"We do not ask that," the war chief of the society said slowly. "We know you can fight to protect the village — you have killed."

Elk could not tell them how much he regretted killing the horse raider, and that his two moons' time spent under the bare sky without robe or lodge had strengthened his belief that all things of the earth and sky were a part of him. True it was necessary to kill game to feed the people — buffalo for meat, but when a man died he returned to the grass which in its turn fed the buffalo. So it was all one great holy circle, a round, as all great things are round — the moon, the sun, the earth's far horizon. With only wild things about him he had somehow been drawn closer to these things, particularly the earth. Several times she had shielded him from eyes that were very near, made him one with her.

There was a scalp dance for a little war party that had thrown some Utes back from the Cheyenne buffalo country. Young Elk could not stay away because he knew that Red Sleeve would be there, but her eyes were for the successful young warriors, and so he wandered past, smiling upon his young sister pretty in her painted cheeks at this first scalp dancing since her young lady ceremonials. At the Horsecatcher's lodge he settled to the fire and asked the old man about the Comanche mustangers.

"They have had very many horses," the Catcher said, meaning for a long time, "and have watched the white man's way with them from the first coming. I went down there when a boy, long ago," he added, making the number of years on his fingers, counting them off in tens — almost eighty years ago. It was when the Cheyennes were above the Platte, before the wars with Comanches started. He visited them to learn something of their good ways with wild horses.

"Ah-h-h," Elk said. "My ears are open to you." He knew that sometimes people of enemy tribes came to the Cheyennes as guests and were treated as friends in the village. He wanted to go as a visitor to the Comanches.

The second mother let her hand fly to her mouth in surprised concern, but Horsecatcher held his silence as he drew on his pipe. Finally he set the pipe down beside him,

128

resting the long stem up against his shoulder. He murmured a little to himself, but nothing more, and so Elk settled to his sleeping robes.

As the horses were gentled, Bear Colt grew out of his coltish jealousy of the new ones, and was willing to stand back while Elk worked with the dun, or with the bay mare and the young race horse that was now called Blue Runner by all who came to throw their wagers down at the betting stick. Sometimes Elk had a helper, the young Beaver Heart, to whom Elk River had become second father. Beaver, only fifteen, was already a bold young warrior with coups counted and a scalp taken, a fitting young son for Elk River and nephew for Owl of the Bowstrings. He wanted to learn something of the gentling hand from Elk, more out of need for good war horses than out of love for them. Yet it was fine to have such a gay, laughing brother work with him, except that when Elk asked him to go out mustanging with him, Beaver became silent. War was what he liked, war and the shy, warm glances of the maidens along the water path and at the dances.

By now the village herds were brought in closer for another move. No people could stay long in one place and remain clean and well, or the horses find grass. Besides, they wanted a place where the buffalo berries reddened their silvery-gray bushes along the stream, and where plums, chokecherries, and wild grapes hung heavy for the gathering. They wanted cottonwoods to stand golden in their lengthening shadows, later to furnish bark for the horses to eat through the deep-snow times. There must be shelter from the biting winds, and water enough to run clear and swift for the robes to be tanned after the big fall hunt.

One bright morning the village started. It was the first gay and happy move in a long time. The Bowstring warriors were now avenged, and the keening time for all those lost in the fight was over. Scouts were out far ahead and all around, and some warriors too, so no one need be afraid. The four headmen led the village, riding in a neat little row and carrying their long pipes. Behind them were more warriors and then the people, with the lodges, the goods, the small children, and the old and worn all on the pony drags that stirred up the dust. The littlest Indians rode in hide sacks from the women's saddles or high on their mothers' backs. Everywhere the women had brought out their finest beaded saddle trappings, their best clothing and ornaments and paint. Young girls like Red Sleeve and even Elk's sister, gay in quilled and beaded buckskin, rode near the edges of the great moving village, while the young men and boys raced their horses back and forth along the sides, showing off, perhaps standing on the galloping backs, or crawling down the tails and underneath and climbing up the ribs, playing jokes, whooping.

Elk, lean and handsome now, and with one of the best riding horses of the village, was not showing off. He was far back, behind the drifting dust, helping with the herds of Horsecatcher, Elk River, and other relatives. They had the horses of the Arrow Keeper's widow along too, always a small herd, even when Gray Thunder was alive. He had been a generous man and kept no more than the least of the lodges, as was proper in one who belongs to the people. The few horses he had kept were all given away in the mourning, but since then Elk and others had given his widow enough new ones so it seemed she need never run afoot again.

Since the flight with the Arrows on her back, she kept a special lodge space for Young Elk, where he could come to sit when his heart seemed low. Sometimes when she was alone she recalled the good days of her husband's youth for the Elk, and the things that fitted Gray Thunder for

130

the life of Arrow Keeper — purity of heart, with the thought of the goodness in all things, and humility, generosity, justice, and courage — a courage harder than facing an enemy, the courage to speak out against a wrong when all the people seemed blinded. Besides these things, the Keeper must have the eye to see the way that all things are a part of the Great Powers, and the wisdom that sits in this.

When others came out to take their turn with the Cheyenne herds, the younger men raced to the moving camp, showing off a little because, while they were known as trusted ones, they were not without daring and fun. Elk was on Blue Runner, full of life from the good ripened grasses, his fine hind legs springy as an antelope's. He pranced, wanting to go, unwilling to have even one nose ahead of him, and when another passed him, Elk made the coaxing sound for speed and stooped low over the mane. The horse shot ahead running with belly low as a fleeing coyote's, almost to the grass. There was a warning whoop or two, and a scattering of boys to the sides to watch the horse pass them all like a blue-gray flying cloud. A thin, high singing cry of admiration rose from the young women, and Elk's throat choked as from the dust. When he reached the headmen with their pipes, he swung far around and started down the other side of the moving village, going like the April wind that sweeps everything before it. Elk knew that men too stopped to look after him, for, although he was still very young, he had already captured the horse that, with good training, could be the fastest of all the Cheyenne nation. Bear Colt might grow into the one with the oddest markings, the strongest-hearted. The dun stallion and his mares would make a little herd tough as the rawhide that not even a hungry coyote could gnaw and that nothing could wear out. Now he had the fastest one too, and that left one more, the finest, the most beautiful one of all, the White One of the south country, to catch.

But before Young Elk had rounded the village completely, he heard the thin shrill cries of approval rise again, this time for a string of hunters coming over a ridge with their pack horses loaded with fresh meat for the evening fires. For this the cries were repeated time after time, and Elk knew how much louder they would be for warriors returning with the signs of victory painted on their faces

"For horses you must also go to our relatives up in the far north, to the Elk River, the Yellowstone of the whites," Horsecatcher said. It was there that Elk's father had saved a colt from the swift-running ice and was given the name of Elk River for it. There were no good catching places up north, not like the spring of the buckskin horses, but Elk should go, look. "There are great herds in the country south of the Comanches, but the strongest herds grow in the country of the big snows, where the weak die young. Stop also at the Running Water plains, see the herds there sweep like wind over long grass, and then cross beyond the Yellowstone for the strange spotted horses of the Pierced Nose people."

So Young Elk traded a pair of good horses at Bent's Fort for warm clothing, and when three visitors from the Northern Cheyennes started back home, he rode along. They were wild young warriors come with their fighting horses to look for conquest and war honors among the enemies to the south, and perhaps pretty wives from the more flirtatious women of their southern relatives. Two had promises from the maidens and the other had three Kiowa scalps, but even so they looked with respect upon their young companion on the spirited riding mare and leading the blue.

They ran into a late electric storm, dry, with great light-ning bolts that turned all the world violet-red and shook it in crashing thunder. Then a steady rumbling rose in the north somewhere and came down upon them — a vast buffalo herd stampeded by the storm sweeping over them. There was nothing for the Cheyennes to do but turn and run before the herd, hoping their horses stepped into no badger holes, to go down under the thundering hoofs of the dark wall that rolled upon them under the blinding skies. They were doing well until the horse running be-side Elk went down, the man's face blank and grayish in the lightning as he pitched forward. Elk tried to stop his terrified horses to pick him up, but the rancid stink of the buffaloes was upon them, the grunting and thunder against their tails, and he could only look back helplessly. But the down horse struggled up and came on as the first of the plunging, heavy-shouldered buffaloes were upon him, the man still on his back.

Elk whipped to both sides to keep his mare up even with Blue Runner, who was pulling at the lead rope from ahead now. Once he thought of cutting the gelding loose to save him if they had to go under, but he would never be found again. Besides, the buffaloes seemed to be scattering a little, the stampede spreading, running out. Soon the herd was separated into streams that moved past under the faded lightning — thinning, slowing streams.

Surely the Powers had looked upon them this night, Elk knew when he managed to find the others alive too. He threw his heart to the sky and the earth and the four Great Directions in gratitude for a moment, and then worked with the worn-out horses. The man who had gone down was hurt, a bone in his forearm surely broken. But that would heal if he was careful. His horse was too lame to ride, a hoof split and sure to crack deeper at every step. So they left him after Elk tied the leg up, off the ground.

On three feet the horse could live in this plenty-grass country. The rawhide strip wouldn't last forever, but perhaps long enough to give the hoof time to heal a little. The hurt man could ride his war mare, but regretfully, for such horses should be kept very spirited.

They shivered through the remainder of the night, and in the morning went on to the Platte with a pack of fat hump ribs from a young buffalo caught in a washout. They built a fire and feasted and then slept awhile, and when they awoke herds of mustangs were coming to water at the river. A half day's ride north they reached the horse ranges of the Running Water country. Elk stopped on a rise to look over the plain that came up to the far blue horizon in all directions. Little bunches of wild horses dotted it as far as he could see, the nearer ones lifting their heads, some running and then circling back in their curious way. Elk had never seen so many pintos, so many of the light sorrels and golden-yellow horses with streaming manes and tails that were like pale yellow clouds.

"Come — we must go. We brought you this way just to make all other places seem poor and without horses," the others said.

That night they camped with some Sioux, long-time friends of the Cheyennes, and were glad to sleep in a lodge, for in the morning the whole valley glistened in the first frost rime of the fall. There was a great deal of curiosity about the fast-looking Blue Runner, but there was no time to take up the challenging wagers thrown down at the betting post.

"If you have trouble giving the blue horse away —" one young Sioux offered.

"I hope to keep the Blue," Elk replied, seriously, "but I should like to go with you on a little horse-catching party to the many herds we saw over east."

"It is more fun to steal them from the Pawnees and the Crows —"

" But then there might be killing — "

" Ah-h-h! " the young warrior said, rubbing his hands together in joy. " But for the wild horses — come back in the heavy snows. Here they are hard to catch other times, the good strong ones, with plenty of water everywhere."

Carrying their gift moccasins from the Sioux girls, the Cheyennes started off toward the Powder River. " These are not shy maidens, these Sioux, not as it is with us," one of the older Cheyennes said to Young Elk's embarrassed hurry to leave. " You will find our young women even more modest than with you."

Elk grinned a little. Red Sleeve wasn't the one he would choose to guide his young sister in modesty either.

The Northern Cheyennes did seem a quiet and reserved people to Elk, particularly after the days he had spent among the boisterous young Sioux, with their loud guttural speech, their practical jokes, and their very fine dancing. He had known many of them before, but that was when he was a boy. Now it was almost like seeing strangers.

There were laughter and dancing among these northern relatives of Elk's, but the Cheyenne tongue, rippling as a gentle mountain stream, seemed even softer here. The chief's harangue to the hunters going out to make a buffalo surround never rose to loudness, although it was very important that everybody work together in this. Their meat-making was still entirely by bow and arrow and spear, with no gun to bring down the occasional buffalo who might break away and lead all the others to freedom. One impetuous youth couldn't hold himself and did almost lose the fall meat for the people. He was overtaken, struck down with a bow to teach him more thought for others, and afterward, when the hunt was done and the meat and robes safe, he was severely scolded in the evening council. But even this was done softly, without one loud word. Young Elk listened and was proud to be a Cheyenne, doubly proud that the soft-speaking man was the brother of Horsecatcher, who was born in the north but married a southern girl and so became one of her people, as was good.

Already Elk had seen some of the wild horses up here, larger and with thicker, longer hair for the winter, and still growing. From far off one horse looked curly all over as a young colt's short mane is curly. Such a horse Young Elk knew he must put his hand upon.

12

*B*UT IN one way these northern relatives were the same. Everybody had welcomed the tall, slight young southerner, come with the good riding mare and leading what was plainly a very fast horse. After the Blue won every race against their young stock, Elk was publicly invited, as a gesture of honor to a special guest, to join a war party. It wasn't just a few wild young men going out on a little raid for coups to please the girls. It was a well-led attack on the Crows, who had stolen some Cheyenne horses and killed one of the herders.

Awkwardly Young Elk refused, knowing how it would be received — this green stick of a youth without a coup to his credit saying "No!" to the polite invitation of a war chief of the Fox society.

Horsecatcher's brother, a prominent warrior in his youth, tried to make a joke of it. "You will excuse our young friend. He is my nephew. My brother of the south is his second father. It is to be expected that our young relative prefers wild horses to all the scalps that the Crows are growing for our warriors to lift."

One of the Cheyennes who had come back from visiting down south spoke out. "The Elk has killed, and killed alone. It was a very strong warrior from a party come to sweep away the horses of the village, with only Elk out to stand against them. He brought the charging Kiowa down to the ground with a rabbit arrow!"

There were murmurs of approval from the circle of warriors, but mostly there was laughter. This young one had killed a Kiowa alone, right at the village, and did not even trouble to carry the sign of it on himself or on the jaw rope of his horse.

So the ill-mannered refusal to join the war party was passed over, yet once more Young Elk had to see what his father and Horsecatcher had both tried to tell him. Everywhere the eyes followed the moccasins of the young warriors, and the soft, warming smiles of the maidens turned toward them.

After Elk got away from the lodge of the Fox warriors, Horsecatcher's sister sent the Crier for him, and when the young southerner came, she put the honored cup of coffee with much sweetening into his hand. "Do not let your heart be on the ground, my nephew," she said. "You have selected the harder road."

Elk warmed to the cup and to the friendliness of the big winter lodge, with the ten, twelve relatives and friends who seemed to live there. The next day some of them took him out to a pink butte overlooking a wide plain. Far off, so far he could scarcely see the color for the blueness, was a herd of horses, and even at that distance they seemed to feel men watching and suddenly ran, wilder than any that Elk had ever seen.

"Wait until the snows lay on from one moon to another. Then they will get tame —"

"You have none like the White One that is told about in the south?"

"There are light grays — we prefer them for winter war parties — but none like the one that the stories of the south speak of."

"Perhaps one can catch those with curly hair?"

138

All could be caught. This was winter country, and some years only the strongest lived, but weak too, and easily captured by those eager to freeze to do it.

Young Elk made the guttural exclamation of approval. This was why he had come north. He would wait if he could be a guest that long.

Next day he helped build a sleeping wickiup of brush and robes back along a bank where other young men slept. He showed himself useful around the arrow-making, cutting and reaming the shafts. He helped with the packing and the move for fall meat, and joined in the hunt too, but only with those sent to spy out the herd and watch its movement. He went with a good old-time buffalo hunter and the two blood nephews of Horsecatcher in this important task — to watch the herd, keep it together as much as possible by well-managed whiffs of human smell from far off, enough to turn them a little upon themselves, but not enough to cause a stampede. This was very important: none of these young herd holders must get excited and chase a buffalo, no matter how tempting, or the hunt would be destroyed, the people lose their winter meat and robes.

The four were watching, strung out well behind knolls and ridges, when the hunting camp flashed the mirror signals that it was stopping two miles away. Then the hunters slipped around in a far circle that was miles across, and began to move inward but against or across the wind, tightening upon the herd, trying to get as close as possible before the buffaloes caught the scent. When the first of the ropy tails went up and the dark, grunting animals began to run, the riders charged into the face of the leading cows, turning them sideways, more and more sideways until they had the herd running in a great circle, faster and faster, the hunters whooping, bringing down those who would break away, until the circle was tight. Their steel-headed arrows and lances flashed very fast, and buffaloes staggered and fell or broke for the open prairie. When the hunt was done, and only some tough old bulls were allowed to escape, over three hundred carcasses lay scattered on the prairie, dead or dying. Already the women and the boys and old men were running in, the butcher knives at their waists gleaming in the sun. Young Elk rode among the dead animals, astonished at the fineness, the density and depth, of the glossy late October coats. The Great Powers indeed clothed the buffalo against the cold to come — cold, Elk had been told, that would burn the breast and freeze the foolish ones, Indians or whites, to death. This then was why some of the wild horses that Elk had managed to creep up on were growing the fine, dark, curling hair.

The young southerner helped his aunt with the butchering, skinning first one side, then turning the fat young cows upon the stretched-out skins to work on the other side and finally to cut them up, piling the meat on top of the open hide on the pack horses. The marrow bones were tied on top, and the entire pack covered by folding the sides of the skins over from front and back. All the while the children whooped and ran among the butchering, playing at killing the great hulking buffalo, chewing bits of the raw liver or tripe. The girls worked busily too, and gaily, or only enough to make their hands seem busy while they whispered among themselves and looked away to the young men, some answering glance with glance, word with word. Elk was in this too, with his pretty cousin, called Cloud, and her friend Prairie White helping with the family kills. For the first time Young Elk saw how pleasant girl cousins could be, not quite sisters, to whom you could never speak directly, and yet not girls whom one seemed to court, or did court, and who tore the heart in two, as Red Sleeve did.

140

"Your southern cousin is quick as a warrior with the knife," Prairie White said to Cloud, and then looked down, ashamed at her foolish words. But Cloud was like Horsecatcher's sister. She laughed. "Why not? It is not that he cannot fight if he wishes — "

For the first time Elk heard such words without wanting to run away, run up to the horse herds, to Bear Colt or farther, to the wild herds. Instead he flicked a bit of cooling tallow over toward the girls and laughed when they jumped away from it, pretending it would be very soiling to their already greasy butchering clothes and their flushed, shining faces.

In the evening the long string of meat horses wound down the sun-yellowed breaks into the valley of the Tongue River, where the smoke of the fires spread in blue layerings that began to lift and scatter in the sign of only a few more days of golden sun. At the camp the meat was unloaded and distributed so no kettle need be empty, and none of tomorrow's drying racks.

Now there was the smell of liver and hump ribs roasting over the coals. Young Elk squatted at the fire of Horsecatcher's brother out in front of the lodge, with his cousins there too for the feast. He thought he had never tasted meat so good. He wiped his mouth and looked over to the council circle in the center of the camp. Here, too, men of wisdom and years of brave work were selected to decide the things for the people, to lead them in everything that they would follow. A moment of choking came to his throat. It was a fine thing, this life of his people, north and south, and he was very lucky to be born to it.

The hunt was made none too soon, or the meat dried and the robes soaked in the clear, cold waters. Before the new moon a light snowing came out of the northeast and turned northward. Elk was told to sleep in the lodge of

141

Horsecatcher's brother because the wickiups would be under snow by morning. In the night the wind rose to a howling, and once Elk sprang up out of his sleep to help hold the shaking lodge from blowing away. The others laughed a little, sleepily. "Go back to your bed robes, Son of the South," one told him. "Our lodges are staked solid."

Apparently it was true, for in the morning the skins were still standing over them, only the top beating against the poles now, for the drifts were very high all around and the first man out the opening had to dig a tunnel through the snow, like the beaver under winter ice.

They ate and slept and played games, often over at the lodge of Horsecatcher's sister, passing the hidden plum pit into the pretty hand of Cloud or her friend Prairie White, laughing when the girls were caught with it. Finally Cloud owed Elk enough forfeits for a pair of moccasins. Her mother looked up from her place near the back of the lodge. "It seems our daughter loses as easily to her cousin as to a young man who is no relation!"

Everybody except Cloud laughed, and then Elk stopped, shamed that he had brought the girl confusion. But soon they were all laughing again.

Often he listened to the old tribal stories from before the days when they crossed the Missouri River coming west, and to those of the exploits here in the north, against Crows and Snakes and some of the Bloods. But mostly they slept, much like the winter bears, until the long moon of snowing was about over, no one going far except to take his turn with the horse herds or in the scout nests around the village. The women went out for wood and water when it cleared a little. Even then the sun played games with them, coming out and hiding again, looking white as a disk of ice behind a veil of flying snow, doing it over and over. Finally the storming seemed past, the drifts hard as stone, the hunting and war horses woolly-haired, gaunt, and hungry, and so they were driven out to some farther young cottonwood groves to gnaw the green bark. Elk was worried about his two southern horses, particularly young Blue Runner, but he was gnawing the glass-brittle bark with the rest.

"Now we can catch the wild horses?" he asked.

"No, not yet. The wild ones know where the wind bares the earth, and they paw the thinner snow away. The next storm will deepen it, and perhaps drift it from another corner."

When the Moon of Frost in the Lodge had passed, and all the war parties caught out had made it home, the hunters started away for fresh meat. They took snowshoes along, to get to the moose and elk yards, places where these animals gathered close against the cold and snow and kept moving to tromp the drifts down. They could be scared out, to flounder wildly in the snow, easy to kill with spear and war ax.

Elk went with his cousins to see this thing, and to look for horses. The snow was so hard he carried the clumsy, unaccustomed snowshoes on his back except in the thawing sun of noon. The buffalo moccasins that his new aunt had made were thick and winter-wooled, with the fur side turned in. They kept his feet warm, but Elk had never felt such cold in his breast before.

"Do not get lost in the blizzards here. You are very new," he was warned.

Elk marveled at the big, long-legged moose, some with horns like great slender-armed hands with the fingers outspread, plunging helplessly into the snow and dying in their red blood gushing from their throats. But even then he was thinking of the dark, curly-haired horses he had seen. If he could get even one —

Yet he had promised his father and particularly Horse-

143

catcher, who knew this north country, that he wouldn't go out on any of his lone horse hunts in this midwinter place. At first Elk had tried to get some of the younger men interested in a mustang party, but it was the coldest winter most of the old people could remember, and no need for horses for war or in courting a wife could draw these young men from the warmth and comfort of the lodge circle. Besides, there was the fun of the winter games, particularly the stick games and the snow snakes, with the warm lodge waiting afterward.

But finally two of the Cheyennes who had been south agreed to go. Because they were experienced men, Elk's cousins were eager to come along. Bundled in their buffalo robes, the five started out horseback. They followed along the barer ridges, taking turns breaking trail with the bark-fed horses. The men pounded them on into the cutting wind, turning their faces sideways too. Nights they camped near cottonwoods if they could and climbed up to break off the newer growth, the frozen green wood snapping like glass. With their horses tied in some sheltered spot to gnaw the bark, the men built a little robe-covered wickiup warmed through the night with a handful of coals. Three days out they began to find some pawed places in the snow, the exposed grass eaten down to the iron-hard earth. They saw several horses that had died since the last snow, old mares and late colts, mostly, and an old gray stallion with great scarrings from his fights to hold his herd, perhaps, and from mountain lions and wolves.

Finally, in the breaks toward the Powder River, where the snow's fall was thin and the knobs are always desert-bare of grass, they saw several little bunches of four, five horses each, pawing for the straggly grass on the upland, working in snow up to their knees. Several seemed very weak, surely unable to last through another freezing night.

The party hid their horses in a protected draw and scattered afoot along a little wind-swept rise that reached up across the drifted prairie. There had been little grass here even in summer, but Elk found ballings of hoof ice and fresh droppings, showing that many horses had followed this rise not many hours ago, not scattered out, but moving one behind the other. He howled a little coyote signal, but the others had seen the same sign. Crow Indians, a large party, and they could have only one aim — the Cheyenne camp — hoping to sneak up through the careless scouting of what seemed too cold weather for an attack.

"It can only be raiders out at such a time. We must run home, warn them," one of the men said.

"Yes, we can cut across the way we came. With luck we may be in time."

Young Elk stood silent in his winter robe. He should go help too, yet if warned in time the camp was far too strong for this Crow attack.

"Is it permitted that I stay and hunt the curly horses?" he asked.

"You are not from this winter country. Sometimes in one hour the blizzard is upon you —"

"Ah-h-h, it is indeed very dangerous —"

But Elk remained. The others left an extra robe with his horse and went on. Elk brought the mare closer, hid her again, and started after the wild herds that had left the pawed places. He hurried, for the days were short. He found a little bunch, their digging hoofs making the frozen snow fly around them, but evidently finding grass. The Elk came upwind, but he was seen from far off. One or two of the horses tried to run, plunging through the crusted snow into deeper drifts, caught, struggling. The others went only a little way or stood watching, all but one weak old mare. She kept pawing the snow, hungry, searching with the urgency of starvation.

There was nothing in this herd worth Elk's valuable time, so he scared those in the snow back to the others and went on to look farther. The sun started down the west, the cold sharpened, and still there was no sign of the curly horses.

It was then that he saw the spotted one. Horsecatcher had spoken of these horses called Pelousies, bred by the Pierced Nose Indians off northwest of the Yellowstone somewhere. He was far away, but it seemed there was one loose here, with a wild herd. Perhaps he had got away somewhere; perhaps he was foaled wild and so there might be more. Suddenly Young Elk was so excited he couldn't tell if the shaking was from the cold or his nearness to such a horse.

He went back to his mare, moved her in as close as he could get by barer ground, careful to leave nothing different from wild horse tracks for the enemy Crows. He camped without fire except a few cottonwood twigs under his sheltering robe. At daylight he started for the spotted horse, over snow crunching and crackling under the mare's hoofs, in cold that burned the eyes and left no sign of life on the sparkling snow. When he found the herd, Elk left his mare and patted snow deep into the wool of the robe belted about him, and so he managed to get closer than he could ever have approached in the south, perhaps because he was coming along the wandering trail the horses had broken, and with only deep drifts ahead of them. The snow still squeaked under his frozen moccasin soles, his breath freezing against the robe flap tied up over his head.

He couldn't see the horse he wanted in their clouds of frost, although he was close enough to distinguish the three red-bays and two buckskins and the mousy-grays under the white riming of their hair. Then he saw the young gray stallion too, almost invisible against the tromped snow, the hindquarters curiously spotted as though a robe, tanned with white earth and beaded in dark spots, were thrown over the horse there. Yet it wasn't the coloring or the thin tail that drew the Elk; it was the head, slender and elegant even in winter, and the proud bearing that was more than a stallion's arrogance, and the strangeness about the horse.

Young Elk came slowly now, starting, stopping, moving back and forth over the snow as a hungry horse might. Suddenly the spotted gray lifted his head and a great snorting of white breath rolled from his nose. It was loud and warning, but even before that the mouse-gray lead mare had started off, running around the little pawed space, snorting at the danger of the deeper drifts, looking for a way to escape. There was none, and so she turned and came pounding back along their feeding trail, her head up wildly, thundering past Elk almost within touching distance. The others came hard behind her, throwing the frozen snow. But they didn't run far, and Elk could see their gauntness under the shaggy, frosted hair, the ice that caked their cut legs browned with frozen blood, the glassy crust where they had passed beaded in red. He turned and followed them, drove them into deeper snow, to lunge through the chest-deep drifts, still crusted enough to bear Elk easily. Several times they stopped to look back upon their pursuer with the red eyes that they would have turned upon a pursuing wolf, as they threatened to charge the Indian, snorting, baring their long teeth.

But each time they went on, and gradually the weaker went down, the colts and two of the thinnest mares floundering in drifts. Still the mouse-gray leader plunged on, until, in her panic, her nose betrayed her and she went off into a drift-covered washout and struggled in snow to her neck. Elk had to harden his heart against the sight of this helplessness as he pushed on after the stallion. When the sun lay red as firelight along the snow, he had him. At the end the stallion didn't throw himself into the hopeless drifts but stood, swaying a little. Elk uncoiled his rope and threw it. The loop settled over the delicate frost-rimed head. The horse jumped sideways and went down, struggling, helpless in the deep snow. By the white darkness Elk had him in a narrow, wind-sheltered pocket with brush enough for a little fire that he must make to save both himself and the horses, particularly the worn stallion, no matter what the danger. All he could do was hope that the Crows were men of sense and were not out sniffing this frozen night for smoke.

There was no cottonwood for the horses to gnaw, but as the snow melted back he pulled a little grass for the horses and chewed a bit of his pemmican. So they got through the night. Three days later he was on the way back with the new Pelousy. He made the friendly sign for the outer nest of camp scouts and stopped a little at their handful of coals to warm himself and inquire about the Crow attackers.

"They are gone — driven off," he was told. "There are two new scalps down there, and some of the others are walking back to the Yellowstone."

Ah-h-h, that was good, Elk said as he ate a little of the rabbits the scouts had roasted, and then rode on to the village. It seemed very pleasant from the winter ridge, the snow worn dark by the many feet at work and at play, the fine blue smoke rising from so many cooking fires.

Horsecatcher's brother rose from his place at the council circle and went out to meet Young Elk. "Ah, you have caught the fine spotted one!" he said, relishing the success. "Your horse medicine is indeed strong, my son."

Even some of the strong young warriors, with many scalps and with coups counted on the boldest of the fighting Crows, came to see, to speak their *hous* of approval. Cloud and her friend Prairie White were out too, admir-

148

ing the horse and teasing Elk about his frozen look, his nose and lips swollen thick from freezing.

In a week he felt fine again. The Pelousy horse was gentled, and Elk was turning his eyes toward the south country and home. Horsecatcher's brother guttered his pipe awhile. "We shall miss our southern relative," he said. "But it seems he has something pulling him, and surely no maiden can turn her back upon him and such horses as he brings home," he said, laughing a little.

The aunt made a soft sound of agreement and then walked beside Elk as he went to leave his good riding mare at the lodge of the warriors who had brought him north. The aunt went along to show her thankfulness to the men who had brought a second son to cheer their lodge this snow-winter time.

Many were out to see Elk go. Cloud and her friend were there too, and brought guest gifts of handsome moccasins. One of the men who knew how much the southerner had wanted a curly horse gave him one, a brown-black two-year-old, curly all over. "She kicks — keep away from the heels," he warned, politely making light of a gift.

Feeling warm and full of happiness for the good hearts he had found here, Young Elk rode away south on his spotted horse, the curly mare and Blue Runner following the lead ropes, the thawing chinook wind blowing at their backs.

13

*A*S ELK RODE southward he felt lonesome after the winter in the big lodge of Horsecatcher's brother, or over where Cloud and her friend lived. By the second day he was getting into warmer country, where the snow was gone except along the flanks of the ridges, still white-patched as a pinto. Although the weather promised to be good and the snowbirds still flew scattered and alone, Elk hurried. All this day he felt he was being followed, and he looked uneasily upon his fine horses, the Blue kept from weakness by the cottonwood bark he had been fed. Even with a rider he was proving stronger than the snow-pawing stallion. But the Pelousy would fatten soon, and Elk could not bear to lose him and the Blue, or even the young Curly Horse, or to endanger them by any fighting. Yet how could one who knew nothing except a little horse-catching, and with only a hunting bow, hope to avoid a fight?

All day Elk had looked for a mustang herd to hide his tracks in theirs, or even a herd of moving buffaloes — something more than the scattered old bulls he found browsing on the barer slopes. He wished he knew the Sioux trails or their usual camps so he could hope to run into a little party or some of their scouts. Several times he delayed long enough to ride the sign of his tribe on some high hill so that friendly eyes might know and signal him in. But there was no response, and by now the fast pace was weakening the Blue, with the Pelousy and the curly mare both dragging at the lead ropes, slow, and stumbling too easily. Once more Elk wished he had troubled to learn the hiding ways of the warriors as his father and Owl had urged.

Truly where the ears are closed the legs must run —

Finally Elk saw the pursuers, five men with extra horses, still far off but coming fast. He turned away from the natural route that buffaloes and Indians followed for easy travel, and the men turned too, and so Elk struck straight ahead to keep them from cutting across on him. Certainly they would not hope to overtake Blue Runner in a race, not if they could have known about him. But they could change horses and drop the worn ones with a herder. Elk could not find it in his heart to let the Blue go, not even if the Pelousy could still carry him.

Twice he took time to creep up behind a ridge to peer over. The second time the men were close, only three left but coming very fast on fresh horses. Even if the Blue could carry him to the hiding dusk, he was too worn out for a run that long.

Then one of the riders went off to the side where he could be seen, to make a sign. Elk began to laugh, for he was riding the sign of *friend,* and then the tribal name, *Cut Finger,* meaning Cheyenne. But in a moment the young southerner realized he had to be careful. Anyone could make this sign just by imitating the ones he had ridden out several times today in plain sight. Elk hid his horses in a canyon and crept to the rim to look. They were truly Cheyennes, two of those who had come north with him, the other one of Elk's own northern cousins.

" Ah-h-h! " one of the men laughed. " If we had been

151

Crows, we would have your scalp! "

" But I left you in the village," Elk said, his pride in the Blue hurt. " How did you come so fast? "

" We knew you would give us a good run, so we each took our three best horses along, your mare too, and sent them back when they were worn out."

Elk felt a little better. The mare — yes, she was tough. " Where are you going? "

The men began to laugh, their teeth white in their snow-burnt faces. " We hear that this is the year of the great elk moving — coming into the sand hills from the north in a big herd like buffaloes, so many they shook the earth."

Elk's cousin would not let this be all. " These two here are homesick for your laughing southern girls," he said. " Besides, they say we make no big wars like your pipe-carrying attack on the Kiowas."

The four camped early and roasted venison that the cousin shot. Perhaps they should rest the horses a few days, here with the grass bare of snow and still very good. They had some Cheyenne relatives not far over east, near where the elk herd was wintering. They might go visiting over there and let the horses fatten a little so they could make a better showing when they rode into the village of the south.

This seemed good to Elk, better than riding with worn horses alone where enemies were perhaps moving. They found the Cheyenne camp in a deep warm canyon down the Running Water. The river, breaking earlier here than up north, cracked like pistol shots in the warm wind of the night. In the morning the ice was water-flooded and beginning to lift and grind on the rising flood and then to pile itself in great blocks of dirty white as the roaring waters overflowed the narrow lowlands.

Elk and the northerners planned to cross over to the sand hills as soon as the stream was cleared a little of the floating ice. But before that the elk herd started north, not in one mass as they had come south, but in long, thin strings, cows, yearlings, and bulls, mostly in little bunches but pushed together in the sand passes and the canyons and then separating again. Young Elk and many others put their horses across the flooded river and watched from high points along the bluffs. The great winter-faded animals streamed down several draws past the watchers. They went down fast, galloping awkwardly against the steepness, particularly the wide-horned bulls, and plunged into the gray flood of the river, swimming free. Here and there one was swept away by the boiling current and washed up on one side or the other, but all except a few weak cows heavy with calf climbed out finally to string along with the rest, up the canyons to the north table-land, and then to slow and scatter into little bunches again.

It was a fine thing to see, although not like the great dark herd that stretched across the whole north last fall, and came running hard, only a few hours ahead of the first blizzard that brought the very cold winter down upon all the country. Usually they came to the long grass country of the sand hills in small bunches and worked back the same way. But either way there was always hunting and meat handy.

Elk listened to the men tell of this, and heard the geese coming in from the south. Suddenly he felt that it was spring and the many moons he had been away from home seemed very long. Who could say what decisions Red Sleeve might have made in this long time?

The others who had been south agreed they should be moving, but back at the camp they discovered that Elk's cousin was not going along. While everybody was out watching the elk pass, he had run off with the young wife of a head warrior. As was proper, the deserted husband

153

sat in his usual place in the warrior lodge that evening, showing no grief, for a woman must be free to go when it pleased her, and the man who showed sorrow, or the anger to follow her, and tried to bring her back, put shame upon himself and her too. Still, it could have been done in a better way than this, less humiliating to both, Elk knew, as he saw the man walk through the village to a little rise at sundown. He did not walk as he had other evenings, for now his heart was on the ground.

From the light in the faded old eyes of Horsecatcher, Young Elk knew he had brought him a fitting gift when he put the rope of the Pelousy into the trembling hand. "Ah-h-h, once, when I was young up around the Yellowstone, a friend took me to the Pierced Nose people, but I have not seen such a horse since."

By now everyone was out to look, some politely, some openly staring under the shading palm to see what this far traveler had brought back.

The gifts in Elk's skin sack were soon given. He had a snow-white ermine for his sister's braids. For his young cousins he brought a chunk of the black glass that made very good arrowheads before the white man's iron came, and was fine for ornaments and for any cutting in the old-time ceremonials in which nothing must be touched by the iron or powder of the white man. Everybody remembered that the sliver of this black glass which Elk wore behind his ear had helped him escape the bindings of the Comanches when he was their captive, and knew that such a gift shared the strength of it. There were little bundles of good northern herbs and medicines for Elk's two mothers, both well known as healers. For his father there was a tight little bag of the inner bark, curled and sweet-burning, from the northern red willow.

"Thank you, my son," Elk River said formally. "Not for

a year have I had this for my pipe. Now the evening fragrance of our lodge will be drawing all the Old Ones to visit, as many as the sweet lumps draw flies! " He spoke very warmly, but the son knew that all the sweet willow in the world was not as much in his eyes as one scalp would have been, one coup.

Yet Elk felt good over the thanks of everyone, and anxious to get away, afraid to ask if Red Sleeve was still a maiden among them, and unpromised. He had a fine string of golden beads that he had won racing the Blue against all the horses of the northerners. These he would keep hidden for Red Sleeve, for some hopeful day.

He did go to stand at her lodge when he saw there were others waiting, a sign that she had not given any promise. The girl came out, and perhaps from long absence her beauty seemed as sun on a quiet pool, with flickerings of golden light. She laughed her welcome to Elk's return, a softer, deeper, more secret laugh. But when all the waiting ones followed her to the dance, her feet were as swift and light as last fall, and her choice of partners as wide.

It was fine in the village now, at least for a few days, with the Crier bringing invitations to Elk to come to this lodge or that one, to eat and to tell how it was with their relatives in the north, and how he discovered the remarkable Pierced Nose horse and about the catching. In the telling of this the two visitors from the north liked to help, making the most of the capture on the frozen snow, although they had to admit that no one was with Elk to see how it was done.

For the first time a few youths followed at the moccasin heels of Young Elk. They offered to care for his horses and brought his family's herd in so he could see how they had wintered, how Bear Colt had grown into a fine, strong young stallion, with the white bear running up his side a fine and powerful sight when the stallion galloped in from the range. He had been kept gentled by Beaver Heart, the new son taken into the lodge of Elk River. The youth was shyly happy with the gratitude and praise of the returned traveler. "Perhaps I can learn some of the horse-catching from you, along with the warring and the hunt," he said softly.

But before the admiration could wear off, Elk was ready to leave again, this time telling only the Horse-catcher's wife where he was going.

She clapped her hand to her mouth in surprised alarm at his words, but she promised to say nothing until two moons had passed. If he was not back then and had sent no message, she must speak to her man about their wandering son. "But only some night when no others are here," the young man begged. "Say, perhaps, 'It is time the Elk were returning from the Comanche country.'"

"This will not please our good man," the woman protested in her mild way, and only mildly, for when a son has done his duty for the lodge and the people, done what is good, then beyond that he is free.

"The Powers have given you strong medicine," she admitted, after a long silence.

Young Elk, more than a head taller than when he was first brought to her lodge, looked down upon Horse-catcher's wife. He smiled a little and shook his braids teasingly. "I always have your good moccasins to carry me from danger."

He went to stand at the lodge of Red Sleeve a little while. The girl came out and laughed softly when he lifted the blanket from his face, so she could recognize him. "It is our horsecatcher," she said, and stood inside the folds of the blue banket a moment. Then she moved to go to the next one waiting there.

"I shall not be at the dance tonight. I am starting south with the shielding dark —" Elk told her.

156

"For horses?" she pouted, meaning not for scalps, for she was still one of the four virgins in the Bowstring warrior ceremonials.

Young Elk knew from the start that he should have spoken of his journey to Horsecatcher or to his father. But how could a Cheyenne say he wanted to slip in with the enemy Comanches, at least long enough to see if they really had girls among them who caught wild horses by overtaking them and leaping from their horses to the wild, free backs. Perhaps he might hear of the White One too, but why should they tell of this wonderful horse to an outsider?

He went out as for more mustangs, on one of the first horses he caught, good, but not valuable enough for an enemy horsecatcher's serious pursuit or to tempt anyone too much. He went to Bent's Fort to visit with some Arapahoes there. They were generally friendly with the southern tribes and sometimes went down south to the little trading post Bent kept for the Comanches and Kiowas near the river the whites called the Canadian, so those people need not bring their families up into enemy Cheyenne country. Although Elk spoke little Arapaho he joined some young men riding south to see what was going on down there. They were a gay lot, one of them a singer, and being at peace with all but a few roving outsiders, they didn't trouble much about scouting or hiding their camp. When they saw that Elk was uneasy, one of them urged that he sing. "Sing, my friend," he said, "sing and forget about bullets and arrows."

The Cheyenne understood this much and laughed a little. "I am in enemy country where some lost relatives in our attack on the Kiowas last year," he explained in his hesitant Arapaho. "They will know that when I cannot talk to them."

"We all must speak with signs to those people — "

"But they will see my moccasins, my arrows — "

"We will say you are our cousin who found refuge this cold winter among the Cheyennes." For the Comanches also treated an enemy like a guest if he got peacefully into the village.

Still Elk was uneasy and wondered if they would reach the Comanches before the spring war pipes went around and the haranguer and the war ceremonials stirred up the warriors, made them hot for scalps. All snow was far behind now. Water birds chattered and scolded in the ponds and buffalo wallows, and a few early flowers bloomed on the sunny slopes, nestling shy and close to the warming earth but hastening, for soon everything might be burnt and dry.

They saw great herds of buffaloes moving northward, their wool bleached and tattered, with many yellow calves among them. The restlessness of the herds, the wildness of the few mustangs, and the sudden flight of birds showed that there were large parties of Indians around, probably shooting meat. Then suddenly they saw a long line of them winding up out of some breaks.

"Kiowas!" Elk exclaimed, and knew that they had been seen too.

So the Arapahoes made their sign and then they rode on. For a while the Kiowas watched, perhaps wondering about the sign, or if they were only advance scouts. Finally the leader started on.

"Big war party, perhaps going into Cheyenne country."

Yes, Elk supposed so. They had enough blood to avenge.

The young men rode a little more cautiously now, passing several meat parties but always managing to keep far away. The next day they reached the valley of the adobe trading post of Bent, with several small camps of Indians off near the creek, their horses over the slopes. And now it

158

seemed that the Arapahoes had more personal business than Elk had suspected. They did not go to the post, but rode straight into the smaller of the Comanche camps, and all Elk could do was follow, hoping that the men who had captured him almost two years ago were far away.

A couple of the young warriors and an Arapaho living in the camp came to greet the visitors. Elk was uneasy. The relative of his companions knew at once that he was a Cheyenne. " Our cousin here is a catcher of wild horses, a man of peace," the Arapahoes explained.

But their relative had married a Comanche woman, and so was now of her people. " Perhaps he is a man of peace," he said, " but what his peaceful eyes see here can be carried to the warriors — "

" This one is not like that."

Elk understood most of the talk, but he was not reassured by it. Yet he was treated like a friend with the others, taken to a warrior lodge and fed and questioned for news of the north, about the buffaloes, and Bent's Fort, and the whole region north of the Arkansas River where the Kiowas used to live and still went, but usually without their families since the wars with the Cheyennes.

" It is very fine buffalo country," one of the old men said regretfully as he drew at his pipe. Fine buffalo country and much cooler in summers. Besides, there was better trading up there, more pay for the robes and more goods for the women to look over, to select and choose from. Women liked that very much.

The Arapahoes, as always, talked for peace. " Your war with our friends the Cheyennes is foolish. You get good horses from the Spanish speakers, to race and to trade. They would trade well up around Bent's Fort."

" Perhaps it could be done," the Comanche said doubtfully. Yet it was true that most difficulties could be made good with a little feasting, some peace smokes, and ex-

159

change of gifts. "There are plenty other enemies for all our young men —"

As Elk walked through the camp the next day, he realized that apparently the Comanches did like to take captives. He had heard that they raided white and Mexican settlements for people as the Cheyennes raided horse herds. The Comanches did this for money, for ransom, but plainly they added to their tribe that way too, whites as well as Indians. He saw several men with plain signs of bearding among them, and many with strong hairing of the upper lip that had been plucked out as the eyebrows are plucked. He noticed two women with brown hair, one with the weak blue eyes of many whites. Several of the Indians used much sign talk — people from other tribes, some who were not married into the Comanches. Perhaps that was what those who had captured the Elk had intended, why they bound him instead of letting his blood flow upon the grass. It made him a little uneasy. Even if those whose horse he stole to escape did not see him, others might decide that he should be kept.

But the Arapahoes were better friends here than Elk had suspected. At least one of them had come to court a Comanche girl, a handsome one with rings on every finger. She had been married for a few moons, but her man was killed in a horse-stealing expedition against the white settlements of Texas. She invited Elk to come with them to a dancing and he had to go, but he stayed back in the shadows as much as he could, ready to jump into darkness if he were recognized as a Cheyenne.

Yet he had managed to get into a Comanche camp, and before long it became known that he admired the fine stories of their horsecatchers here. Besides, he was being helpful, particularly at the lodge of the arrow maker, a very old man who still worked with flint and other stone

160

instead of iron. He made arrows for the ancient ceremonials and for his own hunting, because he must eat no food touched by iron or lead in the killing. Elk saw the man's old eyes come alight when he gave him a nice piece of the black glass from the upper Yellowstone country.

"Ah-h-h, this stone was very valuable for bird arrows in the old times!" he exclaimed, his hands trembling as he turned the piece to catch the light along its fracture lines so he could set his flaker and hammer to it.

After that Elk was asked to go with a party for wild horses before they strengthened with the new grass. He helped in the drive to an old mustang trap in a canyon, just a small drive for the practice it gave several Comanche youths who wanted to learn how it was done. At hunting time Elk helped in the surround of a buffalo herd much as he would at home. By now he had told Arrow Maker that he did not like to go to war, and, shamed by the old man's open acceptance of him, Elk had to tell him that he was an enemy Cheyenne. He did this although he knew that that he would probably be escorted to the edge of the village and from there he would have to protect himself as best he could, without having seen a real Comanche mustang hunt, and nothing at all of the famous sisters.

He was working at the arrow chipping, but awkwardly, when he said it. "I am a Cut Finger, a Cheyenne."

"Yes, of course," the old man replied, without looking up from his work.

Elk was surprised, but he had to add the rest. " I am the son of Yellowstone, the one called Elk River, and a nephew of Owl Friend. Horsecatcher is my father also."

" They are good men, I have heard. Owl Friend I met in the fighting days of long ago. But Horsecatcher — you are then really a horsecatcher?"

"Wild ones —"

It was good, Arrow Maker said. Some had believed their

guest was here to spy on their herds.

Young Elk laughed uneasily that all this had been known, and wondered what more was suspected. He had not come spying on people, or with plans against anything that was made less by taking, by division. He wanted to watch the Comanche horsecatchers, see their good ways, and particularly see the two sisters at work.

Ah-h-h, the old man said, taking a deep breath of satisfaction. "The girls are relatives of my wife. There are *women* in that family."

Elk still slept lightly, and watched for the men who had once captured him, but he felt better, less a skulking enemy in the lodge now that he had named his tribe and all his purpose except his pale hope of seeing the white stallion. Perhaps through Arrow Maker's good words, he was taken out with the Arapaho visitors to the good horse regions. They passed along the edges of much dry country, with wide wandering streams that would sink to sleep in the sand after this swift prairie blooming of spring, until next year. Sometimes the horse herds were as thick as up north of the Platte, toward the Running Water River. They passed a large mustang pen of poles, rocks, and brush in a water canyon, the pen open now, with horse tracks in and out all winter. But when summer came and many were drawn into this wet pocket, the pen could be closed on whatever they wished.

Farther on they had to swing out around a great dusting that came sweeping over the prairie. It was a large party of mounted Comanches chasing a great wild herd into a trap with a double bottleneck, so the horses wouldn't try to back out but, seeing the widening ahead, would think they were escaping. After making camp Elk and the rest rode over through the evening sun. By then the dust was drifting away in a far pale cloud touched to fire along the top.

The pen was quiet, the horses shivering and spent, packing into a tight bunch on the far side of the pen as the Indians approached, their wild eyes burning in the low sunlight. In the morning the men would start taming the best, perhaps fifty head, and turn the others out.

" It is very lucky to get so many together," the catchers admitted. But the water was drying up fast, and they had found these all together at one spring hole. With many experienced men to handle the waving blankets and all well mounted and daring, it could sometimes be done.

Elk looked in upon the horses, some a little larger than up north, and all colors too, but only one dun. There wasn't a spotted horse among them, none with the white patches that the northerners liked so well, particularly white patches on those yellow as sunset — the chief's horses; nor any with many smaller white spots, the horses that the women liked for their handsome ceremonial paradings and for flight, where the spots blended them into the prairie and the canyons.

The next camp the horse party reached was the best one for the springtime, Elk was told, and there they found some Comanches already working. The horsecatching sisters were along. They looked like any other Comanche maidens to the young Cheyenne, but slenderer, a little like the aspens of the north country. They were quietly making moccasins in the spring sun like any Cheyenne girl, except that there seemed to be no beading.

The next day around noon signals came of a horse-catching not far away. Elk and the others rode from ridge to ridge until they saw a rising trail of dust sweep in — a band of horses coming very fast. As they neared him, Elk could see two riders pushing them close, and as the herd passed, a girl on a big gray was racing alongside a fine bay mare that was trying to crowd into the herd, to hide, to escape. But she didn't make it. As they thundered along neck and neck the girl watched her chance, swung over, grabbed the mare's mane, and jumped from her buffalo saddle pad to the bare back. The mare plunged sideways into the herd, but the girl clung close as a burr, pulled the short loop from around her waist, and shot it forward over the mare's head. She jerked it tight and threw two half hitches over the nose, low down, to shut off the wind of the stampeding bay, plunging, running much too fast to buck. As the mare began to slow her furious attempts to clear her back, to run from under her rider, the girl worked her toward the edge of the fleeing herd and out upon loose sandy ground. She was still riding at breakneck speed, the mare staggering a little as her breath seemed to slow, when they went out of sight that way, with not even Elk thinking he should ride to help.

In the meantime the other girl had caught the loose gray and waited, letting the herd go. After a while the sister came back over the ridge, the bay mare lathered white as with the foam of a spring flood. But already she was responding to the rope of her jaw, the pressure of knee and moccasin toe. The girl was dust-streaked, her clothing torn, her hair flying loose, and she looked worn out as she passed the watchers, but she could still lift a hand in greeting. Then, together, the sisters started slowly back to camp, with Young Elk looking after them in astonishment and with the face of admiration.

It was all so swiftly done, so swiftly and so well, that Elk's heart pounded a long time afterward. It was true, as Arrow Maker had said. There were *women* in his wife's family. To be sure, the Cheyennes had some bold and fearless women too, several warrior women, and some who had roped wild horses. But usually these caught the heavy mares unless there were several together to help ride a little herd down. But Elk had never known of any except a Cheyenne man or two making this daring jump in a herd going at a stampeding run, before the horses were worn out. Yet here this girl did it, and barely old enough to have gone through her puberty ceremonial.

Ah-h-h, never would he forget this one. It would be worth a man's whole lifetime to belong even for a little while to the family of such horsecatchers.

14

*E*LK WALKED to the little camp of the horse-catching sisters, with the Arapahoes and some young Comanches along. He hoped to get a few words with the girls, if it could be managed. At the camp they were taken out to the slopes where the young people were watching some racing and games. The sisters welcomed the visitors, let Elk stand between them to watch and to ask how they worked with the wild herds. The girls laughed a little, softly. " Many ways, what seems best," one said with sign talk and the Arapahoes to help. " Some days she has the luck, some days I — "

Elk looked from one to the other, his hands feeling awkward as he made the signs, his tongue confused with the few Arapaho words he knew. But they made him feel better by taking him out to see their own little herd. The new bay mare was already gentled enough so they could walk up to her, and Elk too. They said they preferred matched horses to ride together, like the two handsome bald-faced, white-stockinged blacks that set off their saddle trappings in the ceremonials, and a pair of the big fast grays and two sorrels. They had decided on two bays, and would watch the wild herds now to find a match for the mare they had just caught.

" We like everything together," one of the girls said so-

166

berly. "We plan to marry the same man, when we find him."

"Sisters often marry so among us," Elk said, letting it seem he meant the Arapahoes, certain that the girls were joking, much as the Sioux girls did with strangers, even in this serious tone. "One of you will have to wait, perhaps, for the man to become important enough to have two wives."

"No, we will marry together," they said firmly, shaking their braids, laughing a little at the young man's doubt of their seriousness. But that night he danced with them both around the fire in the bright moonlight, exactly the same number of times with each one.

"We are told you are a good horsecatcher," one of them said.

Elk wanted to speak of Bear Colt and the spotted Pelousy horse, but he stopped before he made the betraying words, for it seemed important that he pretend here, although everyone seemed to know that he was a visiting enemy. He wanted to ask about the White One down here somewhere, but he could not say the words, not let them think he was here to take the best of their wild herds and afraid, perhaps, to hear them say that they knew about the white stallion and were waiting to find a match for him.

The girls needed no urging to talk of horses, not even of a certain ghost horse, white as moonlight. They liked to talk to this stranger who seemed more interested in horses than in scalps and coups. They took him to the home cooking fire for the evening meal. It was fine, and the moonlight was late when Elk started back from the little camp with the others, having to listen to a little teasing about the horse sisters. But on the way two men suddenly jumped from the shadows before Elk, shouting; "Cheyenne horse thief! Cheyenne spy!" and grabbed for him, a knife gleaming in the moonlight. But Elk had already ducked and,

167

leaving his loose cotton shirt in their hands, slipped between the two men and dove for the shadows along the
trail with the Comanches hot after him. As he ran he
realized that these men must be of the party that had captured him when he was looking for a horse for the fleeing
wife of the Arrow Keeper. They had spared his life, and
in return he had escaped with one of their good war horses.
It was plain why they were angry.

But a man must save himself, and Elk managed to out-
run them now by dodging through the shadows of the
late moon, but then he heard horses coming from two directions and knew he would really have to be sly as a
weasel to get away, so far down in the strange Comanche
country and without a bow or even a water pouch.

He ran for the dusky breaks, keeping to the shadowed
ravines and telling himself how foolish it was to get caught
outside of the village here and the guest protection it af-
forded. By dawn the young Cheyenne had more reason for
regret. The Comanches were really after him, at least fifty
riders searching all the country, scattered out, appearing
along this draw, that canyon, looking from every ridge,
near and far. Once more Elk needed to know the tricks of
the warrior to enable him to slip through the rings of
watchers angered as though by blood. They must think
him a spy, perhaps spying for a coming Cheyenne attack
such as the one that the Kiowas and some Comanches suf-
fered at Wolf Creek. They might even suspect that he was
the one who was down in the Kiowa country before the
attack, and not realize that it was to bury his brother.

Elk knew that if he was willing to hunger and thirst he
might be able to hide so well no one would find him until
the buzzards began to circle over his remains. But he
hoped that with luck and slyness perhaps even a horsecatcher could escape the Comanches and their region before the buzzards had to come.

He recalled how easily they had captured him with their little decoy fire. That trick would not trap him again, but he wished he had his gray calico shirt that he left behind in their hands last night. It was a good hiding color, better than the gleaming brown of his skin. Yet dust would help in this, and patience, the patience that grew out of the long waiting at the water holes for the horses. He looked all around in the brightening daylight for a place that was good, one that would not be a Comanche kind of place but one of, say, the northern people, Elk's northern relatives. But he must decide quickly. Once seen he was lost. Then, as he started out of the top of a long ravine, he saw a man riding across the tableland very near, and so he dropped into a narrow little ditch, not much over two hands deep, and half full of dead weeds and grass. If the man happened to ride close by, Elk was lost, but perhaps the hole was too small to draw anyone to look. Besides, there was nowhere to run now except back into the ravine, which would be searched.

With his face down so his eyes could not draw anyone to look, the young Indian waited, his ear full of the steps of the Comanche horse, then the sound of another from farther away, and much talk as they came together at the ravine, one down in it, the other along the edge. Elk would surely be discovered if this one came much farther and looked to the feet of his horse, or the animal shied.

Yet all Elk could do was wait and hope that his medicine was strong today, feeling the bit of black glass tied behind his ear press against it, the sharp sliver that had helped him cut loose from Comanche bonds once, and might be strong for him again.

The Comanches searched carefully, poking lances into every brush and weed clump, into every hole, as one worked up the bottom of the ravine the other along the upper edge and out upon the table, closer and closer to

169

Elk until he was almost within touching distance. Once his horse snorted a little, and Elk held himself unbreathing, but it was apparently in the other direction, to where another rider came up on a ridge and signaled, for the Comanche replied and rode past. Long afterward Elk still lay motionless, afraid they would return, perhaps led by some lone moccasin track to this hiding. The sun walked up the sky and down the other side, and Elk was like one in the long wait for a dreaming, a guiding vision.

At dusk he finally moved out, his knees cramped, his legs so stiff that they refused his weight, and for a little while he had to crawl before he could stand and head northwest. Although the thirst within him was like a fire, he had to turn from the region of water and keep to the hard-ground country that would embrace no mark from the passing moccasin — land so dry no one would expect to find a man afoot and without a water bag anywhere upon it.

He traveled all night, with no dew to soften his moccasins, but the soles wore through anyway, and the next day during his hiding he had to think of how he could save his life. His tongue, thick and dry, filled his mouth, thirst gnawed at him, and bright lights moved before his eyes. He tried to watch the sky and the horizon a little for the sudden rise of a bird over enemies moving, and even more for some sign that might mean water — some darkening growth that his eyes might learn to see, or some wandering animal or bird. He dared not hope for what was so unlikely in this drying season: a darkening of the pale sky, some cloud that was more than a thunderhead to climb up and then blow foolishly away into the whiteness of a flying mare's tail against the blue.

But Elk was far from the signs that he understood and from the guiding of the bird that lives with horses, far from all creatures that needed water to live. He saw the pretty tracks of a desert turtle and of a snake or two and some lizards. He caught one of these and ate it raw for the juices, forcing it down his closing gullet. He saw several little birds that rose fleeing from his moccasins, and once a buzzard circled far off in the east and then drifted out of sight.

When it seemed that he must run like a wild creature for water, run until he fell with outstretched hand, he slipped out of his hiding to find one of the fleshy cactus that he had seen. He singed it well and then crushed the pulp and sucked the sickening water from it. But his stomach rolled like a snake under his belt and retched.

As the sun bent toward evening Elk had to dare being seen. He sought out another cactus with its bit of ugly water and then moved on. From a scrub cedar at a tip of rimrock he cut a short spear to throw at a rabbit if he struck some grassy ravine where one might live. He watched for something to make a little hunting bow and some arrows, the points hardened over a handful of coals in some sheltered washout. He watched for buffalo bones too, although there were no trails, no buffalo chips anywhere among the sparse bits of sagebrush. Yet he still hoped to find a little water and was looking for an old horn to carry some along on his way over the dry stretches beyond, for he must keep up in the dry country, far from the Indian trails that climbed northward in the great steps from water to water.

He followed the thickening line of a stretch of rimrock, although the stones of it cut his bleeding feet, hoping to find some plant that might mean water near in the ground, and plain enough for a northerner to understand. As the evening deepened he found a patch of the large white evening flowers, and once the thorns of the bean bush clutched at his leggings, the bean bush that Horsecatcher had said was seldom more than the grazing travel of a horse from water, not over five of the white man's miles. As the late moon rose, he watched carefully for more of the bushes, trying to decide on the direction that water had lain at least part of the year. He found no more, and so went back to the first and turned westward on the moon's path. Suddenly he saw something dark and large as a squatting buffalo — the shadow of a whole clump of the thorny beans and then several more beyond, until finally a low place opened before him, white, bare — the sandy wash of a stream that ran water perhaps once or twice a year, from cloudbursts or a little snow higher up.

But as Elk crossed the dry sand, still warm to his swollen feet, he noticed a hole that some water-seeking creature had made. He fell into it, digging with both hands until he felt moisture, and then he began to throw sand like a badger before a pursuing wolf. By the time that the sand was soggy and seeping a little, the young Indian was weak and so sick he had to lie back. He held himself so a moment, looking up to the thin moon and the darkness around the shining horns of it, all a part of the Great Powers of the earth and sky and everything that lies between.

Slowly Elk let himself drink a little from palmfuls of the sandy water. Then he took out a few roots he had dug on the way but could not eat with his mouth dry as a withered hide. He tried to gnaw at these awhile and drank a little more water, not too much, for even the wise lead mare must learn to hold back when she and her herd have thirsted overlong. Then the Elk went back into the low bluffs where he could watch the empty dry wash and slept as he had not since the night before he went to visit with the horse-catching sisters of the Comanches.

He went to sleep thinking not of the men searching for him, but of the sisters. There would be a lucky man someday, the man that the sisters selected as their husband.

✿

The next day dawned hot even before the sun, but there was water deep as the wrist of his hand in the hole, and tracks of little creatures that had been drawn to it. They made the young Cheyenne feel warm and happy that he was part of these small ones in this good way. Yet his need drove him to kill a rabbit that lived in the low bluffs beyond the wash. Afterward he found an old buffalo carcass and gathered up the pieces of dried hide to soak in the water of another hole dug into the sand. From these he made rude moccasins for his swollen feet and a water bag, and had enough left for a short rawhide string.

That evening he started over the north tableland again, toward a low ridge of hills standing blue against the far horizon. Grass appeared in brownish patches, then in greener stretches where a little snow had perhaps lain in a late storm, and finally there was buffalo sign. He found a bull dead only a short time, perhaps killed by lightning. Here he made a passable rope by soaking the hide that the wolves had pulled back from the belly before it rotted. The next day he saw a small herd of buffaloes, six cows and several calves. With the little rope handy about his waist he tried to creep up on a calf, but they were well guarded. The next herd was larger, quieter, and more scattered for a hot, still nooning. Here he crept up very carefully, wondering in his slow snaking from hollow to weed clump if he would be doing great wrong in this killing. But it seemed he must have the skin, the meat.

As Elk neared, the yellow calf shied and started up. The Indian jumped for a hoof, held on, and cut the bawling throat, prepared, as the blood gushed out over his hand, to run downwind when the mother charged. She came, head lowered in a roaring rush, but she lost Elk's dodging scent and stopped in confusion, nose up, trying to smell what her eyes were too poor and too hidden in wool to see. Elk whooped and started the lead cow running and the others after her, the mother too. Before she could return he had dragged the calf over a little bank, downwind, and as more buffaloes thundered past she was drawn along.

When the herd was gone and the dust settled a little, Elk skinned the calf and stripped the meat into thin flakes to hang like heavy brown rags on the weeds to dry. Working with the green hide stretched over a rock, he cut all but the thick hump section into one long strip, beginning at the edge and going around and around. Then he pulled the green strip out straight and smooth and let it dry that way, to be braided into a rope later. The thicker hump skin he dried over a little hole of embers to make it stiff and hard for moccasin soles, the way warriors made their shields from hump skin and old bulls. Properly dried, they could turn arrow and spear and even a glancing bullet.

By now Elk planned to need many moccasin soles, for he might be out many moons. He had a certain horse in mind, the ghost horse, as the Comanche girls called him, white as moonlight and very difficult to see on the dry, burning plains. They spoke sadly of another such horse down among the Spanish-speaking people, but he was never to be caught either. When he was pursued too hotly by riders numbering at least ten times the fingers, he was cornered in a good place, with high cliffs rising on three sides and a deep canyon on the fourth. As soon as he saw he was cut off there, he turned his panting, spent face to his captors and then plunged like a falling white bird over the canyon wall. When the men looked down they saw that nothing could live through such a fall. He was down there, dead, and already the buzzards were circling while the bold men rode sadly home.

"We did not see this, but it is told so," one of the girls said.

Elk had murmured his sorrow. He knew about a white
174

stallion that Horsecatcher had tried to trap when he was a youth. The first time he got an arm broken in a big chase for the white one, and when he was cured and took up the pursuit again, he was caught in a tornado and lifted off the ground, with trees and brush and animals too all flying around with him. He was found almost dead, and when he recovered he made a thankful offering at ceremonial time and let the white horse go, which was never seen again. When he talked of this to Elk his old face had seemed very far away in the firelight.

"There are few white horses; most are light gray —" he had said, as though to destroy the youth's curiosity.

"This one we know about is white," the Comanche sisters had said. "White as the snows that live in the mountains, but it is known that he cannot be caught."

Elk made a meat and marrow bone hole from the calf, with hot coals in the bottom, covered by a thin layer of sand, the meat in the paunch, then more sand, more coals, and finally sand over the top, so there would be no betraying, no beckoning meat smell. He regretted this, for the odor of fresh meat roasting was almost as filling as the meal.

But the meat was very sweet, and as the young Cheyenne ate he thought of the first time out alone to catch a horse. It seemed very long ago now, almost half a lifetime, these two years since he caught Bear Colt. Now he planned to search out the finest of all, the White One, white as moonlight, white as a great cloud standing against the sky.

The next morning the young Cheyenne carried along everything that he could. In his hands was the length of new rawhide rope, stiff, but to be worked into some softness as he traveled. The moccasin hide and the dried meat tied to his back made a bundle big as the baby a woman

175

would carry so. There had been more meat, and this he cached for emergency use, if he were driven back this way by enemies.

With a little water bag at his belt and the meat, he could push in closer to the drying springs and water holes, take chances. He was tall as his father now, but lean as the war lance from the horse-hunting life and the hunger and thirsting of his flight from the Comanches. His feet were well moccasined and his long braids wrapped in protecting rawhide, but his breechclout and leggings were worn as those of a man in great mourning, although the young Cheyenne's heart was gay.

Twice the Elk saw fresh sign of Indians, and so he knew that he was drifting too close to the spring war trails and drew farther back into the dry regions, seeking the white horse and the trap that the Comanche girls had described. There were a few horses around now, although the remote streams were mostly curving beds of dry sand fanned out like yellowish snow blown this way and that. Elk had no idea where he should look, trusting to luck, and hoping to find the little bird that lives with horses. Once he came very close to a lone mare foaling and had to decide whether to catch her and tame her to ride. It would take a day, perhaps, and she was old and weak. Besides, the new colt could not keep up for a long while and he would have to kill it. He had killed the buffalo calf, but that was for food —

As he considered this, there was the sudden flight of a bird over him, the bird that lives with horses, but there was no song to welcome the Indian hidden in the grass, no song of courage, nothing except the rush of wings, and so the young horsecatcher rose and slipped around the mare and on his way.

Once he saw a prairie fire far off but running fast before the northwest wind, bringing a dark galloping herd of buffaloes and deer before it, coyotes and rabbits and smaller creatures too, until suddenly the young Indian was surrounded. But he made it to a creek bed through the flying cinders and smoke and buried himself in the sand, still moist, while the fire swept over him. He came out coughing, to find two cottontails cuddled down where his digging had uncovered wet sand. They must have run a long time, for they were so tame he could pick them up and stroke their fur, both scorched a little, an ear tip of one burned so the edge felt crisp between his fingers while the rabbit burrowed into hiding under the Indian's bare arm, the long hind legs pushing, pushing.

When the ashes of the sparse grass cooled, Elk carried the little rabbits to some rough breaks that the fire had skipped and set them free. They huddled together a moment, strange and afraid in their sudden freedom. Then the Indian spoke: " Run, little brothers," he said softly.

One of them scurried away, but the other huddled against the comforting moccasin, and with a smarting in his eyes Elk picked up the trusting little creature and set him down a ways off. Then he clapped his hands. The rabbit fled, the young Indian's laughter following him.

The next day Elk struck a fine little valley. It started around a sagebrush bend somewhere and spread out into bottomland, with brush and trees and a little creek that widened into water holes and then led southeastward and spread again. There it joined what looked like a wide stream bed coming in from the north but white in sand now.

The young Cheyenne lay flat in a clump of sage looking carefully over all the far horizon. He waited a long time, holding himself still as his eyes searched out everything, every whirlwind or sun glint that might be the far signal of smoke or mirror flash. There seemed nothing, and finally he dared study the valley below him, with horses

177

nooning around the drying, mud-edged holes. Several shaggy buffaloes ruminated on a knoll, and two deer were going up along a brush patch, but there was no white horse anywhere.

When Elk was satisfied there was no enemy sign, he moved around the ridge to a little fork that ran water in the spring but now was a sandy bed through a close-cropped little flat. It headed up in a steep, tight, brushy little box canyon. There were around twenty-five horses there, clustered together, drinking, switching flies inside what looked like the narrow open end of a pen.

Elk's heart began to pound as he made himself study the wild place very carefully from his hiding. The old Comanche mustang trap was wonderfully located and made. With good preparation one man alone could close it, temporarily at least, with no more than a rawhide rope and perhaps a shirt, if he had one, or his leggings hung on the rope to give him time to pile up stones and brush for a solid walling.

Elk looked down over the horses, a good mixed herd but without a one of light color. Then his eyes caught something moving up against the outcropping of rocks. A horse barely discernible against the pale stone started down toward the water, stopping every few steps to lift the head, finally to stand out white as a gleaming cloud before the brush and trees. The fine carriage, the mane and tail like mist blowing in morning sun were surely of the white stallion that Elk had heard described all the way from the Cheyenne camps of the north to the Comanche sisters. It must have been such a horse that killed himself by a leap over the cliff, and so this White One might do if he saw himself trapped.

For the first time in his life Elk really wished for help, for many fast horses and experienced men like Horse-catcher and Yellow Wolf — a great party of good Chey-

178

ennes, or at least one or two men like the dead Two Wolves. Perhaps best of all would be the Comanche sisters.

But Elk stopped himself there. Comanches were what he did not want here, Comanches and Kiowas.

As the white stallion came to the water, the other horses moved back. He drank alone in the pen and then galloped out upon the little flat, running as a colt runs, for the joy and the wind, swift as the pale lightning of summer heat, yet white as blizzard wind and as strong, and barely seeming to touch the worn earth. Elk thought of what the Comanche girls had called him — the ghost, the spirit horse.

"The other one went off the high rocks like a flying bird," they had said. "None can catch such a horse."

Elk pushed his face into the earth, making a vow. He would catch this White One; he would ride that noble back, the back of the ghost horse of the Comanche country.

15

*E*LK KEPT hidden all that day, and when the evening came and the horses drifted off to feed, he moved in closer. He worked cautiously, washed himself in the muddiest of the water holes and then walked carefully on the dried humps of mud to leave no track for any spying Indian. Above the springs, away from the pen, he settled down for his long wait and planning. With most of his meat safe in a dry cache, he prepared to hold himself back from all impatience, no matter how much danger there was from the Comanches who might come to their trap, or from those heading through for the north.

It was much like other times, Elk knew, except that here he must plan the moment to close the old pen, and how to do it, without the preparation that would leave man smell around for the sharp nose of the mustang. With all the water outside there was no way to force the horses into the pen. Only the shade of the trees and the freshness of the water drew them.

Because the Elk's shirt was back in the hands of the Comanches, he plaited a mat of grass and rushes and slept on it for the human smell. The more he studied the pen the more it pleased him, and as the creeks dried there would be more and more horses around. He wished he had a little of the salt he had carried for the first stallion he caught. With that he might really get a large herd, and greedily Elk began to dream of needing more rope, at least something strong enough to make hobbles in addition to the hair rope he could braid from the manes and tails of the poorer horses to be turned loose again. But he stopped himself from such thoughts in shame, for surely this was defilement. It was the white stallion that he wanted, the one that even Horsecatcher believed could not be touched by the hand of man. Down there he was standing away from the other horses, with a strangeness about him that the rest seemed to feel.

The Elk settled to watch for enemies and to study the habits of the horses, the white stallion always in his mind, awake and sleeping, until he became something like the white buffalo to the young Cheyenne, the white buffalo that was the sacred animal of his people.

After almost a whole moon's time waiting for an opportunity, hoping to see the good time to close the pen without losing the horses, it was suddenly there upon him. A little cloud had risen in the northwest, but this one did not grow into a great thunderhead to ride the sky, flash with red and yellow, rumble in earth-shaking threats and then blow away. Instead, the cloud spread out low down, coming dark as a grazing herd of buffaloes, slowly, quietly. Late in the afternoon it began to rain. With this to wash away his sign, Elk ran out to tie his rope to a tree at one end of the pen's gate. He covered the tying well and then laid the rawhide along a trough that he cut with his knife across the opening, his sleeping mat tied to the center and all of this covered with earth and smoothed by the pattering rain. The free end of the rope he drew into a brushy thicket and dug a hole there just large enough for him when he squatted down, with everything hidden in the brush to look untouched.

After it was done Elk hurried to a little bank up under the rim of the canyon and stretched out on the dry, warm sand. As the rain moved on he slept, to be awakened by voices that seemed part of a dream. Then he held himself unmoving. At a fire just below him, twelve, thirteen Comanches were huddled around a bright fire, bright for drying out. They were so close that if one of them got the fire glow out of his eyes he could look up and see the shadowy form there under the bank. The Elk could not escape, for any movement would surely be seen, and so he held himself still in the sudden chilling of the night.

Several times the men pushed the long, drying sticks farther into the coals, to burn up bright again. Once a herder went out to a little slope where horses were grazing, and another came back to squat at the fire.

For a while it seemed that the men would not settle down at all, but when they had drawn the drying coals well over their sleeping ground, they rolled into their blankets. Once a man came through the starlight to look all around the top of the canyon and over the tableland. He walked so close that Elk could have reached up and touched his moccasin, but he went on, and as soon as the fire died down the Cheyenne slipped away, thankful that he had buried his rope down there very well. Then he remembered the little brush-covered hole in the thicket —

What a foolish one he was! Almost a whole moon's time he had sat here as though there was nothing under the whole sky except a herd of wild horses. No, one wild horse that was white as morning mist.

The wet earth is known to be friendly to the moccasin and cherishes every track, holding it so plain that even the blind can follow. But Elk had to escape without leaving his beckoning trail behind. With a stick he tested the ground ahead of him in the dark, feeling it out lightly to

182

leave no sign as he searched for rock or sod for his feet. By dawn he was overlooking the fork of the creek below the pen, in a patch of shaggy weeds, watching. After a while he heard horses running, and for the first time it occurred to Elk that these might be horsecatchers — men come for the White One — and a choking of fear and sorrow rose in his throat.

But in a little while the Indians rose up on the tableland, strung out, leading war horses, headed north. Elk counted them carefully, fourteen, but he watched the bottoms and prairie for a long time for sign of someone left behind. No bird rose in disturbed flight, and the wild horses coming in to water showed no uneasiness. Toward evening Elk went back to the pen, moving carefully. At the dead fire he counted the sitting places, fourteen. But the Comanches would probably return this way, or later parties might be following. He must work fast, as soon as the wind was right.

By the next evening Elk had the pen closed. He hid in the covered hole through the day, until the herd was quietly nooning in the shady pen. Then he jerked the rope up, with the mat flapping from the middle of it. The White One and the rest, about twenty, reared back, snorting, crowding against the rocky pocket that was the far end of the big pen. Elk tied the rope well but as in a dream, scarcely believing that the strange white horse had not escaped before this. Perhaps he would go as soon as he saw the opening closed by more than a silly rope that he could leap as he would a cobweb swinging between rosebushes. Yet for all his doubt and uneasiness, Elk worked as fast as he could, piling brush and trees and rocks across the entrance. Several times the lead mare moved up warily to snort at the rope and mat and whirl away at the man smell of it, while at the back the white stallion stood folded upon himself, looking back over his shoulders at Elk, his great dark eyes never moving from the man-creature there, steady and burning.

Finally Elk had the opening closed as high as he could reach and it seemed all that was left was the catching and gentling of the White One. Some of the others too, the best, including the white mares, which were truly light gray and not the gleaming snow of the stallion. They would make good winter horses for the northern relatives, for all their storm moons when drifts lay white over everything. But as he looked at the fine animal standing remote from the crowding herd although touching them as they moved uneasily, what Elk thought of was the face of Horsecatcher when he brought the White One home — the old face shining as with firelight upon it.

" It was very certain that no one could catch the White One alive — " he would say in great wonder.

Elk started home, his heart swelling within his naked breast so it seemed it must burst the cage of his ribs and the cover of lean, bare muscle and brown skin. He, Young Elk, had captured and gentled the ghost horse, the White One, and was taking him home along with the best of the herd he had caught, all side-hobbled against fast running but free to feed and travel. He had had little trouble catching most of the horses after he closed the good Comanche pen or hobbling them with rope made from the tails and manes of the culls. Even the very fast-looking lead mare tamed well.

Then, after a day of fasting, he laid his first hand upon the White One. He had left the stallion for the last, almost as though he had to give the uncatchable one every opportunity to escape. By that time the horse was lean and hungry, and used to the Cheyenne working among them, moving so quietly, making his friendly, coaxing little song as one horse after another lost the fear of his hand. Finally, when Elk was bent down readying his rope to toss a light loop over the fine head, the horse came forward. Elk felt the movement behind him and stiffened. If there was meanness in the White One, he could kill an Indian here very easily.

But instead of the slashing teeth, the striking hoofs, there was a soft snorting against Elk's back, and a drawing away. The young Indian held himself still and soon the head neared again, the breath soft against his hair, snuffing it, and the touch of a rough, wet tongue testing the dusty braid, the brown ear, and in that moment Elk felt soft and dizzy, his heart a flying creature with the joy of this.

But there were serious problems in this strange country, where the young Cheyenne knew nothing of the grass and the water holes, nothing beyond his proud possession of the White One, the ghost horse as the Comanche sisters had called him. He wished once that he could take the horse south to show them, see the amazement on their strong, quick faces. But Elk had to keep his fine horses alive, and for this he must move eastward to lower ground, near the old, old summer trails used by Indians going north and south ever since man first came to this ground. Besides, there was no way to hide the tracks of driven, unmounted horses, or the curious pattern made by the side hobbles. He kept up the drying streams as high as he could, coming down only for early morning watering after he had searched the horizon carefully for the thinnest wisp of smoke from a cooking fire. In this way he crossed the country of the Canadian River and was nearing the Arkansas and the country beyond it, where he could hope to run into Cheyenne parties as surely as Kiowa or Comanche.

Then one early dawn he was awakened by a movement in the sagebrush beside him — an Indian creeping to the

185

high point to look over into the little pocket of Elk's night camp which he had left, as always, for cautious sleeping. It was a Kiowa scout, within reach of the knife in Elk's belt, the silent death song of the knife that could perhaps protect his life and his horses. But Elk could not kill, not even to save the white stallion, and he let the Kiowa creep away and run for his horse, to signal to a party passing far to the east, a very large war party, surely headed for the Cheyenne villages to avenge last year's attack where so many were killed.

Elk slipped down the washout to his riding mare. It seemed that he had not been seen, nor his hidden horses, and surely the scouts at home would warn the people. He would wait with his hidden herd, his White One, and start homeward again tomorrow by a roundabout route. But as he reached his mare, he saw a second party following the first, leading war horses too, and he remembered that at this time of year the Cheyenne villages would be separated into small camps for meat, many men away hunting after the long winter, or horsecatching, or in war parties to drive out the enemy tribes pushing in upon the buffaloes. The Kiowas might well surprise one of the camps — probably Elk's own, because it was usually farthest south, wipe it out, particularly with the blood of last summer's attack on the village to avenge.

So there was no choice: he must ride hard to get home ahead of the war parties. But he could not leave his horses hobbled on the prairie for the enemy, and helpless before wolves and mountain lions. He did not let himself think of the White One at the mercy of the first challenging stallion. In his hurry Elk let himself be seen by one of the scouts, who immediately made the riding sign for *enemies seen.* The second party turned and rode hard toward Elk, and he whipped to his herd in the canyon, stooping down as he passed each horse to slash the hobble with his

186

knife, the horses scattering in alarm at the charge, until there was only the White One. There Elk got off and put his face a moment against the warm neck. Of them all, this was the only one he had never ridden, and he was glad that he had finally known it must be so. Now he cut these hobbles too, and with a whoop started the herd away. The stallion whirled and followed too, his mane a cloud of shining mist about his noble head.

Elk could not bear to look back as he started up the snake-head canyon, his eyes blurring with water, not even when he heard the far, whooping signal that the Kiowas had seen him. He let the gray mare out, hoping that the party would be held up by the good horses of his herd, knowing they could not catch any of them here. But he would have to hide as cleverly as the striped young of the quail, with a party ahead and one behind.

He looked back from a rise where his pale mare would be lost against the rising white clouds of a thundering day. He saw some of the Indians ride after a couple of the half-tamed, hobble-stiffened mares, while the rest came on. He dropped off the other side of the ridge as falling over a bank and was gone.

Free to travel fast now, in country he had crossed several times, once with the widow of the Keeper of the Sacred Arrows, Elk headed for Bent's Fort, to fool his pursuers. Then he struck straight for where the camp should be by now. He pushed the mare as hard as he dared, riding all night, as the warriors could not, unless they wanted to enter a fight with tired horses.

Next afternoon he found the camp, and from a high hill he sent in signals of many attackers coming. Men ran for their horses and charged out to meet him, while signals and riders were sent to neighboring camps. By sleeping time everything seemed as usual, yet ambushes had been prepared in several good places, Elk with the most likely

187

party, to scout, not to kill. In this he was firm, and none spoke against it now.

As expected, at the first whiteness of dawn the Kiowas came through the breaks toward the mist-filled valley, some charging for the horse herds out several hills away, others heading on silent hoofs toward the village sleeping on the misty bottoms. But they were caught by arrows and bullets between a brushy rock in the valley and a warrior-filled ravine. Two fell, their horses stampeding. The rest whirled, fired a shot or two back into the arrow-sprouting mist, and whipped for the breaks, but there was firing from there too, and so they scattered and fled into the fog. It was so thick that they got away, but they lost their traveling horses left with the horse holders, who gave up when they were surrounded, with several of the good war chargers too. The men that had fallen, one only a boy, were found wounded and brought in with the others. They told what the plans had been and joked that they had cost Elk his fine catch of mustangs.

" It was a good herd that he had? " Horsecatcher asked, and in reply got the sign of twenty — two times the two hands, and the sign for very, very good. " And you would not have seen him if he had kept hidden and not hurried back to the horses, to free them? "

The young man had everything very well hidden, one of the Kiowas admitted. But it seemed that bad luck lay upon their expedition from the start, another said. Nothing had been well prepared. They had hurried away to do a little avenging fast because the chiefs were planning a peace conference with the Cheyennes. They planned it through the Arapahoes, with the Comanches in it too. It was to be a peace eternal as the earth, the headmen were saying. They wished to save the fine young men of both peoples from the need of early death.

" A peace conference! " Elk River exclaimed. " It is well

that no death blood was spilled here today!"

There was another reason for their bad luck, one of the Kiowas said, laughing a little at himself in the Kiowa fashion. The medicine of the young Cheyenne with the horses must be very strong, for he had captured the white stallion of the south, their ghost horse. He had let himself be caught, but only by a man whose desire to warn the people was so strong he let the White One go.

"The White One? Not the white stallion of your south country?" Old Horsecatcher said, rising in his amazement. "And our son let him get away?"

"He cut the hobbles and sent him flying."

Horsecatcher sat down slowly, his faded eyes on the youth he had taken into his lodge as a son. "It was a hard choice, hard as the rock of the Yellowstone country of his fathers," he said.

Ridge Tree, the medicine man, worked well with the wounded Kiowas, and next morning they were ready to start away with presents and good horses to carry them home, although this tribe usually needed no such gifts from anyone. Even though they had come raiding the village, they were treated as visiting headmen now and escorted out upon their trail by a gay delegation riding behind the Cheyenne chiefs.

"Tell your people our hearts are good for peace with you," Owl and the others said, and as the Kiowas started off a trilling song rose from the young women watching, Red Sleeve among them, and Elk's sister White Moccasin very pretty in her excitement.

Afterward there was busy preparation to receive the peace delegations coming from the south, and in this Elk could only try to keep out of the way and not think about the sorrow of letting the white horse go. He went to sit at his mother's lodge, but they chased him away too. "All

189

except the very lazy ones are out hunting meat for the coming feasts," she said.

"Or at least for horses," his sister added, laughing, her eyes past Elk to their mother, as was fitting and proper with this grown brother.

"It is plain that one is not wanted," he said, ducking out ahead of the half-sewn gift moccasin that his sister threw at him. When he got off a ways he met a group of girls gay and laughing as all the village seemed to be except Elk. He loosened his rope and swung it gently sideways to settle over Red Sleeve's neat head. He nestled it about her shoulders and then jerked it down, but still gently, and yet holding her arms to the sides of her beaded dress. She stood still, as if waiting, and to this all the Elk could do was toss the end of the rope toward her, making dips and waves in it as it ran to her, almost alive, so good was this one with his lariat. Then he ran away toward the horse herds, brought back from the hiding for the Kiowa attack, hurrying as though to head off some wild mustangs with his man smell, while the girls shouted after him, taunting.

"You have learned very bold ways from the Comanche maidens, it seems!"

He went to look at his best catches among the family herds, the dun stallion and the mares, two with yellow colts, and some other yellow ones that the dun had fathered, the dun he was naming Two Wolves for the dead brother now that he would never catch a White One for the honor. There was the fast Blue Runner too, and the Pelousy, fat and as fine as though garbed for a ceremonial. Standing off a ways was the big black Bear Colt, which his second brother was training, not for war, but as Elk had promised the little colt at the catching, for a medicine horse in the parades and rituals. Elk whistled and the Colt came, to stand holding his handsome black head down for the

190

war bridle. Elk looked at his side with the bear, a great white bear now, still running, and was half eased by this first capture for the loss of the one that was white as mist and no more to be held in the hand than a cloud is.

Perhaps if Elk had been willing to kill the Kiowa who discovered his night camp, he would never have been seen and the white stallion might have been saved. But there would have been blood in his village circle, death falling upon them out of the mist, and the tender young peace between the people would have died before it was born. Who could tell what might have come from that one stab of his forbidden knife?

A messenger interrupted Elk's visit with his horses. There was a call in the village for him. Elk turned uneasily to the brother of his lodge, and the youth grinned. "Go," he said.

But it was not for a victory celebration or an invitation to eat at some pretty girl's lodge. Those were for great warriors, not for a young man who would be only a horse-catcher. Instead Elk was taken to the lodge of the widow of the Arrow Keeper, and there, to her questions, he told her of the white stallion.

"He touched me first —" the young Cheyenne said, speaking a thing that would have been immodest before all except this one with whom he had faced the long death. To such a one a man speaks the truth without shaming his face. "He came to me in the pen, before a rope touched him, smelling and then licking at my hair, my ear."

"Ah-h-h," the Keeper's widow said softly, "perhaps it is the sign of great things to come if you keep your moccasin tracks in the simple, worn path of the people."

Outside, the father and Horsecatcher and two of Young Elk's uncles were walking in dignity around the evening village circle. The Crier running ahead of them beat on his drum and shouted out his news, his invitation. "Come!

Everybody come to the lodge of Elk River. There will be meat for all! "

Then, when the people were outside the lodges, standing, looking, the Crier came past the place of Gray Thunder's widow, calling for Elk to come to the feast. Behind him walked the two men who were so large in the life of the young man, his father and his second father. This time they circled the village alone, singing. First Old Horsecatcher:

"There is one of new name among you!
One who has brought riches to the herds,
Honor and protection, and the hope of peace to us.
To him I give my name, Horsecatcher! "

Then Elk's father sang too:

"I am giving our son my name also.
A strong young man, one to make the heart leap.
We give him our names together:
Elk River, the Horsecatcher! "

The young Cheyenne stood in the doorway of the Arrow Keeper's widow as in the confusion of a dreaming. Everywhere people came running up, crying their joy, the young women too, Red Sleeve the first of all to make the trilling song of praise.

Suddenly everything softened in the Elk and once more in his breast there was the feeling of flying, a very great flying that seemed far up against the white cloud of the summer sky.